THE NEW ADVENTURES OF

FOSTER FADE

THE CRIME SPECTACULARIST

FEATURING STORIES BY

ADAM LANCE GARCIA
DERRICK FERGUSON
AUBREY STEPHENS
DAVID WHITE
H. DAVID BLALOCK

FOSTER FADE THE CRIME SPECTACULARIST
CREATED BY
LESTER DENT

PRO SE PRODUCTIONS
2014

A Pro Se Press Publication and a Volume of the Pulp Obscura Imprint

Edited by - Tommy Hancock and Morgan Minor
Editor in Chief, Pro Se Productions - Tommy Hancock
Submissions Editor - Barry Reese
Director of Corporate Operations - Morgan Minor
Publisher and Pro Se Productions, LLC-Chief Executive Officer - Fuller Bumpers

Pro Se Productions, LLC
133 1/2 Broad Street
Batesville, AR, 72501
870-834-4022

proseproductions@earthlink.net
www.prose-press.com

Cover Art by Mike Fyles
Book Design, Logos, and Additional Graphics by Sean E. Ali
Formatting of E-Book by Russ Anderson

The New Adventures of Foster Fade the Crime Spectacularist
is a work of the PULP OBSCURA imprint.
PULP OBSCURA is an imprint of Pro Se Productions and is published in conjunction with titles from Altus Press collecting the original adventures of lead characters featured in PULP OBSCURA titles.

TABLE OF CONTENTS

ADAM LANCE GARCIA

DEAD MEN'S GUNS

AN ADVENTURE OF FOSTER FADE
THE CRIME SPECTACULARIST

Chapter I
THE BARREL OF A GUN

THE MURDER WEAPON arrived in the post two days before they found the body. Innocuously addressed to *The Crime Spectacularist, 40th Floor, Planet Tower,* the weapon had been packed in a box filled with yellowed copies of the *Planet*, pages dating back long before the first Foster Fade column. A .45 Colt—the sort one associated with the Old West—the murder weapon had only a faint gunfire residue, but was otherwise clean, giving little evidence. The serial number had been filed off and the inside of the barrel drilled out. It wasn't uncommon for the tabloid to get mail on Fade's behalf; with such wide circulation Fade had made a number of admirers and critics, but until now, no one had mailed him a gun, let alone one used in a murder.

The victim, a gangster named Brandon McMillan, was discovered in an alleyway in Red Hook, a single bullet wound to the back of the head, execution style. His body had been unceremoniously buried beneath a pile of trash, and would have remained there had the hot summer sun not done its job to ensure the stench of decay filled a full city block.

Another gun arrived a week later, a Colt Super .38, its serial number filed off and the barrel drilled out. Wrapped like a birthday present in three year old copies of the *Planet*, the gun came complete with a typewritten note listing the number "2" as well as the gun's make and model. The body—another execution style killing later identified as local Mafioso Michael Capitelli—was located a few days later in SoHo, propped up against the wall as if he had been taking a drunken nap.

Three weeks passed before the third gun arrived, once again packed with yellowed copies of the *Planet*. A Mauser Model 1934 Pocket Pistol, .32 ACP. The gun, like the previous two, had its serial number filed off and the barrel drilled out. The handle had been worn down smooth from overuse and had a significant amount of gunfire residue. The note inserted was similar to the previous, the number "3," the gun's make and model, but this one came complete with a quote from one of the earliest articles on Fade: "Fade swears to hunt crime, in all it's forms, until the City that Never Sleeps can at last rest easy."

And an address.

Fade rubbed his chin as he gazed at the guns lined up in the center of his desk, unable to ignore the small pit that had formed inside his stomach. Though the third body was yet to be found, all evidence was pointing to a psychopath, the first of Fade's career. Taking out goons and thugs for the sake of circulation was one thing, but men who were driven to kill by their very nature were another matter entirely.

"I know you're not the most popular person in the underworld but, even I think this is a bit much," said Din Stevens, Fade's ghostwriter. She was seated on the plush modernist couch on the other side of the office, a curl of platinum blonde hair falling over her eyes. Her lips were coated in a fiery red, off-setting her pale skin.

"Popularity takes all forms, my dear," Fade commented. "Sometimes even scary forms."

"Here's to keeping my name out of print," she said, lighting a cigarette.

"I hate to break it to you, but it's not that much of a secret that you're my ghostwriter."

"They know I'm a blonde, so I'm going brunette."

Fade smiled wanly. "Not sure that'll work for you, dearest."

"My hair, my rules." She took a long drag of her cigarette. "When do you think our next body is going to show up?" she asked, smoke pillaring out of her mouth.

A buzzer sounded from Fade's office door. Sliding aside a small hatch on his desk, Fade peered into the end of an intricate periscope. Looking out into the hall he found Captain Evan Stern standing outside the door. Fade frowned and placed a small box over the guns. "A few minutes ago. You might want to start taking notes," he said with an off-handed gesture to Din as he walked over to the door. "Our circulation is about to jump another thousand."

Din shimmied her platinum eyebrows as she silently reached over to the side table and grabbed her notepad and pen.

Fade opened the door and Captain Stern walked in. Even though he stood well over five feet tall, Stern seemed minuscule compared to Fade's near seven feet. He kept his cap low to obscure the wine stain birthmark that covered the left side of his face. A thick walrus mustache hung over his lips; shifting and bristling like a hairy caterpillar.

"Mr. Fade," he said, smartly extending his hand.

"Captain Stern," Fade said, ignoring Stern's hand and placing his own in his pockets. His relationship with the police was cool at best. New York's finest didn't much care for the idea of a newspaper employing a gadget man to act as gumshoe, and thus treated Fade like a second-class citizen. Fade knew he ought to turn the other cheek and be the bigger man, but then again at his height he already was. "Where was the body found?"

The officer blanched. "I would be of the mind to ask you how you knew that, but—"

"But they do call me the Crime Spectacularist," Fade cut in with a grin.

"Not even a real word," the officer grumbled under his breath before saying, "Our victim was another gangster name of Kevin Howard, one of Pete Barry's boys. Found him slumped beneath a fire escape in Harlem right off—"

"Right off Eighth and One-Forty-One, no?" Fade finished for him.

The white of Stern's face began to match red of his birthmark. "How in the holy hell do you know that, Fade?"

"Which leads us to why I called you here," Fade said triumphantly. He spun around and moved behind his desk. He drummed his fingers against the sides of the box. "When we spoke on the phone yesterday I told you there was going to be a third body found. You seemed pretty perturbed by the suggestion and called me some choice words, many of which aren't repeatable in mixed company, and two of which I don't think were English. But here you are."

"Cut the dramatics and get to the point, Fade," Din sighed. "Gubb hates it when you go purple."

Fade cleared his throat and revealed the three guns with little flourish. "Voilà!"

Stern pointed to the guns while his mouth worked for a response. "What the hell are those?"

Fade looked at the weapons with a frown. "Guns. At least that's what they look like. I can never tell."

"A .45 Colt, a Colt Super .38, and a Pocket Pistol, .32 ACP? These calibers match—"

"Match the ones used in your three murders, yes," Fade said

condescendingly. "Do you have any other major revelations you'd like to throw at us?"

"Why the hell do you have these?"

"Well, they were mailed to me. I have strange fans."

Stern let out a slow, steaming breath. "Now tell me why I shouldn't arrest you for withholding evidence?"

"Besides the fact that I'm too pretty for prison? Because up until the moment you walked through the door I had no real way of knowing for certain that any of these had been used in a murder." He scratched his cheek. "Though I'm not sure what else you'd use guns for… Hunting deer?"

"Fade—!"

Fade slid over the typewritten address that had come packed with the third gun: 214 West 140th Street.

"It's almost like I have a third eye for—What the hell are you doing?!" Fade exclaimed as Stern snapped a cold-metal handcuff over Fade's extended wrist.

"Withholding evidence is a crime, Mr. Fade," Stern said in a low growl. "I don't know how it works with others, but with me that sort of stuff gets you put in jail."

"Didn't we just establish that I'm too pretty for prison?" He looked to Din. "Would you mind interjecting or at the very least say something exonerating?"

Din shook her head as she wrote furiously in her notepad. "Nope, this is way too good."

Fade sighed. He didn't want to play this card, but… "Captain Stern. Clearly there's been a misunderstanding; one that I'm sure will make for some really great reading. The mugs are going to love it. Especially Police Commissioner Horton, who I know is a fan. I took a photo with him just six months ago; you can see it framed over my right shoulder there. No, my right, your left. There we go. Anyway, I'm sure the mugs—and Commissioner Horton—are going to love the part where you arrest me, Foster Fade, the Crime Spectacularist, the world famous detective who, through no fault of my own was mailed three possible murder weapons, and upon realizing that these guns were valuable in your investigation, offered my assistance, free of charge. So, please slap the other cuff on me and let's see how high my readership goes… And how low your career ends up."

Stern's face was something out of Dante. He glanced over to Din who had already burned through five sheets of paper and was moving on to number six. The captain cursed under his breath—something about blackmail being against the law—before he unlocked the handcuff and hooked it back on his belt.

"Now, where were we…?" Fade said pleasantly as he adjusted his shirtsleeve. "Ah, yes, poor Mr. Kevin Howard."

"Don't think it's some gangland killing? They tend to do that a lot," Din commented dryly from the other side of the room, her gaze never leaving her notepad.

Stern gave Din a tepid look. "Regardless of what you put in print, we're not that thickheaded."

Din snorted despite him.

"Care for a drink, Captain?" Fade offered as he walked over to his dry bar. "I can usually guess someone's drink just by looking at them." He glanced back at the police captain and gave him a crooked grin and a wag of his finger. "You look like a gin man. Tell me I'm wrong."

Stern let out a haughty sniff and raised his chin to Fade's offer. Fade tutted and shrugged, pouring himself a glass of bourbon on the rocks. He didn't bother offering Din a glass; she was working.

Fade swirled the glass around, the ice melting in long, twisting waves. He took a sip and rolled the amber liquid over his tongue, savoring the burn. "So where did you finally find the bullet?" he asked without looking at Stern.

Stern's mustache bristled in a mix of disbelief and displeasure. "'Found' is a big word, Mr. Fade. 'Found' means we had to go looking for it. Fact of the matter was it was sitting right in front of us." His jaw worked as he tried to find the right phrasing. "We dug it out of the victim's skull," he said at last.

"And you brought it with you," Fade said with a smile. He held out his hand expectantly as he walked over to the police captain. "How nice."

Stern glanced down at Fade's hand while his own unconsciously brushed against his pocket. "What makes you think that, Fade?"

"You wouldn't be here if you didn't need my help, Captain," Fade said with an arched eyebrow. "I don't need to be a genius to figure that out, thank you."

Stern huffed. "Didn't know you were one."

"That's what it says on my business card, at least," he said with a nonchalant shrug. "'Foster Fade: Crime Spectacularist and Genius."

The 'and' is an ampersand, but you get point: If it's in print, it must be true. If it wasn't, I'd be sued for libel and we wouldn't want that, now would we?"

Stern ignored Fade's quip and gestured towards the three guns lined up on his desk. "Maybe I want to see the little collection you've got going."

"Maybe, but you didn't know I had it until now. And you and I both know that won't help you," he said, holding out his hand.

Stern let out an exasperated sigh, fished into his pocket, brought out a roll of gauze and handed it to Fade.

Fade thanked the officer with a sideways grin and a bow of his head before unraveling the gauze with flourish. He held the bloodstained slug between his forefinger and thumb, and brought it up to the light. "Hm," he sounded. "A .32 caliber."

"Fits your number three pretty perfectly," Stern said, nodding his chin at the guns lined up Fade's desk. "And it confirms that your pen pal and our murderer are connected."

Fade took a deep breath. "Just because the caliber of the bullet and the gun match doesn't mean they're a couple. There are a lot of Mausers in the city, Captain Stern, as I'm sure you're aware." He turned the bullet around several times before placing it carefully on the desk. He then slid open his bottom drawer and brought out a .32 caliber Beretta. "Oh, don't worry, Captain," he said due to Stern's expression as he removed a bullet from the magazine. "I have a license for this one somewhere in here, I'm sure. Do me a favor, could you pick those up?" he asked, indicating a stack of books piled high on the floor with a distracted wave.

Stern's brow furrowed beneath his cap. "Excuse me?"

"The books," Din answered dryly, her pen zooming across the page as she transcribed every single word. "He wants you to pick up the books."

Fade put down his Beretta, picked the Mauser up off the table and loaded in the .32 caliber bullet. "Hold them out in front of you in a line like this," he instructed, holding his arms out to demonstrate. "Parallel to the floor, if you could. Ten should do." He then glanced at the Mauser then at the stack of books and frowned. "Make that twelve."

Stern looked back and forth between Fade and Din before he hesitantly acquiesced, pressing the stack of books against his chest. "What is this for?" he asked, turning to Fade.

"This," Fade replied, firing the gun.

"The hell are you doing, man?!" Stern howled, dropping the books to the floor and drawing his sidearm.

"Calm down, Captain," Fade said placidly. He placed the Mauser back on his desk as he knelt down and began leafing through the books one by one, a bullet hole wormed straight through from cover to cover.

"I could have you arrested for shooting an officer!" Stern shouted, spittle flying.

"That'd be true if I'd shot you, but by the looks of it the only victims are dead men." Fade tossed the books aside one by one. "Twain, Byron, Dickens. Aw…" He held up a copy of *The Canterbury Tales*, a hole drilled halfway through. He propped open the book to find the bullet standing in the middle of the page. "It ended on *The Miller's Tale*. I was looking forward to reading that one again." Fade pried the bullet free and examined it closely as he got to his feet.

"Fade, you better tell me what the hell you were trying to do before I sling cuffs on you again and haul you in, the press be damned!"

"Proving a point. Catch," he said, tossing the bullet at Stern who caught it clumsily. "Tell me what you see."

"A goddamn bullet."

"Look harder, Captain," Fade said impatiently, picking up the bloodstained bullet off the desk. "What's *on* the bullet?"

"A bunch of scratches."

Fade looked at Din and smiled. Din rolled her eyes.

"'A bunch of scratches,'" Fade repeated sarcastically. "If that's the way you want to think about them, sure." He walked over to the other side of the office and pressed his foot against a small pedal. There was a brief sound of gears cranking to life. The wall slid away and a table rolled out with a microscope atop it. He turned on a small light at the base and placed his bullet on the slide. "When a bullet travels through a gun's chamber it's etched with very unique lines. Think of them as a gun's fingerprint, no two are alike." He beckoned Stern over with a curl of his fingers.

Stern hesitantly holstered his standard issue .38 and handed Fade the second bullet.

"Our killer is smart, or at least he thinks he is. Not only is he using a different gun to kill each victim," Fade continued as he placed the second bullet besides the first so that their bases lay flat against one another, "he's also scratching out their serial numbers and removing the gun's fingerprints."

Stern leaned forward to peer through the microscope. Fade didn't need to look to know what Stern was seeing: two bullets nearly identical, pressed back to back, one with uniform parallel markings, the other with an additional set of rougher scratches, concealing any similarity between the two. "How is he doing that?" Stern asked.

"A drill—at least, that's my assumption." He gestured to the guns on his desk. "The inside of the barrels are a mangled mess of inconsistent grooves, which might indicate a drill. I doubt it could be anything else."

"Which means there's no way to prove whether your collection and the murders are connected," Stern concluded, his mustache rocking back and forth.

Fade nodded, a satisfied smile in the corner of his lip. Stern was catching on. "Or for that matter why he's killing these men in the first place."

"Could be an assassin," Din said with a shrug, "seeing as his victims have only been gangland thugs."

Fade shook his head and began pacing the room. "Plausible, but unlikely. Assassins have been known to leave calling cards, but they don't exactly go looking for publicity. And mailing your murder weapon to the number one columnist—no, not columnist—number one press-hired detective in the world isn't exactly what one would call subtle. This guy has a vendetta—or believes he has one—which is why he's mailing me." He paused and turned to Stern. "We have to face the fact that there are going to be more victims before we stop him. You have to understand: He wants to be heard."

Din smiled grimly as she flipped to a blank page. "Then I guess we better start listening."

Chapter 2
FAN MAIL

THOUGH HE WAS off by two thousand, the *Planet* circulation jumped as Fade predicted. The murders had become the talk of the town, with two more occurring over the last month. The fourth victim, Matthew Weglian, had been found three weeks prior, sprawled out on the subway tracks below 34th Street, a gunshot wound to the back of the head. The other papers, prestigious and otherwise, had begun looking for a psychopath to call their own in a desperate effort to bump up sales, thankfully to no avail.

Owner and publisher Gubb Hackrox threw the latest copy of the *Planet* on to the conference room table. "'The Post Box Killer Strikes Again,'" he said, pointing to the headline, a bit more proudly than Fade cared for. Gubb then looked at Din sharply. "That was my idea. Going on the record for that one. Sure, he doesn't use the post box to kill, but the mugs who read us aren't the brightest bulbs on the chandelier."

"If it really is a 'he,'" Din commented, her cigarette hanging from the corner of her lip. She looked over the copy and frowned. "You forgot to proof this sentence. It should read: 'The fifth victim, David Guida, was found stuffed *in* a drain pipe.' It says 'stuffed *on* a drain pipe.'"

Gubb waved this away. "'On,' 'in;' you shoulda proofread it yourself, lady. Besides the mugs won't notice. Bless 'em if they can read and not look at the pictures like it's the goddamn funny pages. Man or woman, the mugs reading us keep on spikin'. A few more weeks of this and the *Times* and *Herald-Tribune* are going to go out of business. You should see the letters we have coming in. They love this guy—or gal—running around taking out criminals. They say no one likes a vigilante, but our numbers are provin' 'em wrong." He glanced at Fade, who was walking over to the window. "What's wrong with you? Your stock jumps with every new paper we sell."

Fade touched his forefinger to his lips, watching the miniature people flow through the streets in rivers and streams. He had five guns now, a High Standard Model "B" and a Fabrique Nationale Model 1900, both following the pattern of scoured serial numbers and drilled barrels, now added to the lot. As before, the notes that accompanied them had the number of the victim alongside the make and model of the gun and the location of the body. It was the killer's choice of quotes, however, that had grown increasingly more disturbing. Just as the first had been a quote from one of the earliest stories about Fade, these had been pointed statements taken out of context, giving his hyperbolic, high-minded words a darker, malevolent spin. "Crime, in all its forms, falls within Fade's crosshairs, and his aim never waivers." "The victims, murdered as they were, only hinted at the vile depths to which Fade's enemies would go." Fade pinched his eyes shut, seeing the words typed out across the back of his eyelids.

"There's going to be another murder soon," he said aloud, as much to himself as to the others.

Gubb furrowed his brow as he lit up his cigar. "Should we feel sad?"

Fade gazed at Gubb reproachfully.

"He's got a point, Fade," Din said. "Your pen pal *is* killing the bad guys. Last time I checked that qualifies him as one of the good ones."

Fade placed his hands in his pockets and sighed. "And what happens when he stops being so picky?"

Din shoved her cigarette into the ashtray with a twist of her wrist. "Psychopaths usually follow a pattern. Jack in Whitechapel liked to cut up girls. Ours just happens to hunt the scum of the Earth. We should count ourselves lucky."

Fade threw out his arms. "Look, I'm not saying I'm sitting around sobbing over the deaths of a bunch of gangsters. Hell, they already like to kill themselves as it is. We're better off with less of them running around, but they're *still* people, some of them even had families. Our… Post Box Killer," he said, the name somehow tasting wrong on his tongue, "is starting to set a precedent and not a good one. We don't stop him soon, it'll open the floodgates and people will start thinking it's a decent idea to go out and kill people without any regard to the law. No one likes a vigilante?" He tapped his long index finger against the conference table. "This keeps up we'll have a city full of them."

Din took a deep breath and her eyes dropped to her feet, conceding the point. "Fine," she said. "What's the plan? You usually have one of those."

Fade arched his eyebrow. "Do I? Here I just thought I was flying by the seat of my pants."

Gubb puffed his cigar and shrugged. "As long as everything makes it into print I don't care what you two do, so long as it's interesting."

"Don't worry, Gubb," Fade assured him with a grim smile, "we'll be sure to keep it entertaining."

THERE WAS A distinct smell of diesel as they dragged him through the darkness. At least he assumed it was darkness, for all he knew it was bright lights and neon signs outside the burlap sack. He could hear the strong men beginning to grunt from exhaustion. Fade was a narrow piece of work, but at his height even skin and bones started to weigh a man down.

The sixth gun—a Remington 51—had arrived a week ago, mailed in a shoebox stuffed with clippings of the first Post Box Killer article. The note, which Fade had now come to dread as much as the drilled out sidearm, had cut him deep. Containing a quote from his and Din's second article, the killer made his stance clear: "Fade's mission may not always be condoned by those of you reading these words, but know that he is always fighting on your behalf." The police had found the victim shortly after, a hoodlum named Alfonso Brown, propped up against a lamppost just south of Harlem, a bullet to the back of the skull.

Fade's captors' footsteps began to echo back. They were somewhere big and empty, which was never a good sign. They lifted him up, tucked in his knees and dropped him down onto a wooden chair too short for his legs. A moment passed before the burlap sack flew off Fade's face, white spots and silhouettes slowly resolved into a dozen distinct people standing around him in a large pool of light. Fade recognized a few: Joe the Barbar, Frank Costello, Bumpy Johnson, Willie Moretti, Joe Adonis, Pete Barry, "Lepke" Buchalter, James Nord, and Bugsy Siegel. The other faces rang a bunch of bells in the back of his head, but the names escaped him. Other fedora capped men stood in the shadows, Tommy guns slung at their sides.

"All of you just to see little old me? Jeez, you sure know how to make a girl feel special. I'm about to blush."

"Thanks for taking the time to meet with us, Mr. Fade," Pete Barry said, stepping forward, "seeing as how we don't usually get along."

Fade smiled pleasantly. "Hey, as long as you read the *Planet*, you're a friend of mine. And seeing as we're all friends you mind undoing these ropes?" he asked, holding up his bound hands.

Barry looked behind Fade. "Johnny, could you?" he said with a wave of his hand.

A six-foot-ten enforcer, who Fade recognized as Johnny "Wits" Pomatto, walked over, switchblade in hand. "Don't move too quick," Pomatto said in a baritone, the blade flipping out. He gave Fade a toothy yellow grin. "Don't wanna cut you," he said before slicing through the rope around Fade's wrists in two quick motions.

"Thank you kindly," Fade said with a nod, massaging his wrists. He looked to the mob heads surrounding him and felt something turn over inside him. If the killer's goal had been to further organize organized crime, he had succeeded in spades. "Well, seeing as we're all here together in this epic meeting of the minds, someone want to offer me a drink or are we going to have to go straight to business?"

"First thing I want to get out of the way," Costello said, crossing his arms. "Tell us honestly, Mr. Fade, you the Post Box Killer? Would make life a lot simpler if you just came out with it and saved us all the trouble."

Fade leaned forward, resting his right hand on his knee. "Yes, I arranged this whole meeting to confess my crimes. Do you have a priest on hand? I'd like my last rites, because I'm about to die from a case of infectious idiocy. Symptoms include shrinkage of the brain and drooling of the mouth. It's viral, so you all might not want to get to close to Mr. Costello there; he's our patient number zero. And Johnny Pomatto here just got a big ol' whiff of it. No offense, mind you, but there must be something incredibly stupid floating in the air if you honestly think I could be *that* insane."

"You about done, Mr. Fade?" Nord asked, his sallow face looking like a Death's Head.

"I've got a few more witticisms lined up, but we can save them for later."

"Tell us what you know about the Post Box Killer that we don't," Buchalter said. "And for the sake of time, keep it short."

"Fine," Fade said with a shrug. "Nothing."

"Don't try and pull our leg, Mr. Fade," Barry said. "You're the one this freak has been mailing his pieces to."

Fade gave him an exaggerated nod. "That's right, but I take it you haven't been reading the *Planet* too closely, have you now? Outside the guns, the notes, and the location of the bodies, I'm just in the dark as you all. More so, probably. It's very frustrating."

The mobsters glanced at one another in turn, their faces a mixture of apprehension and doubt.

"It's not that we're short on men, you understand, Mr. Fade," Johnson said. "We'll always find someone to pick up a gun fer us. It's just bad for morale, you see. First we all thought it was between us, the usual business, turf warfare and whatnot."

"Almost like he's taking one from each of us," Costello added. "Like he's trying to send a message."

"We don't need someone going after us that's not supposed to," Moretti added. "Cops, you, we understand that. We don't like it, but we understand it. That's how this game works. But some nut bag running around taking us out like we're deer for the hunt? That's just not gonna work fer us."

"Must be hard for you," Fade said with a little more than a drop of sarcasm. "Listen, fellas, I'm loving this psychoanalytic session, it would make Sigmund Freud real proud, but let's skip the Oedipal complex, and get to the part where you tell me what you're going to do for me so I can do something for you."

"We're not killing you," Nord said, running a finger over his lips.

"Point taken. But that's not enough to solve this little mystery we've got going."

Nord regarded him with his coal black eyes. "No. No, it ain't."

Fade crossed his legs and steepled his fingers. "Let's start simple. There has to be a connection between the victims, a through line that links them all together. If we can figure out what they had in common, we might be able to work backwards and find out who our killer is." An uncomfortable silence filled the space as Fade's hosts waited to see who'd speak up first. Fade impatiently cleared his throat and began to stand out of his chair. "Look, if you don't want my help, I could easily—"

"Buddy, if there was a connection," Costello cut in, "you'd be the first to know."

Fade massaged his eyes. "You mean to tell me that outside the whole aspect of them all being 'criminals', there's nothing connecting these six victims." The mobsters shook their heads or nodded—depending on their preference. "Nothing at all? They didn't all graduate from Little

Mobster School together, play 'kill the coppa' beneath the Brooklyn Bridge? Dammit," he cursed at their blank stares. "Why can't it ever be simple?" He ran his hand through his hair as he began to pace in one small circle, thinking aloud. "All right, fine. One thing we haven't been posting in the paper is the fact that all the victims were killed, or at the very least, found close to their homes. That's one thing we know for sure. So either our killer is stalking his targets or he already knows where to find them. But how could he know that? You all wouldn't happen to have some kind of a phonebook listing you all this guy might have stolen?"

"The only way anyone could know where these boys lived is if he's in the business or he got his hands on their records," Pete Barry offered.

Fade stopped short and spun around. "Wait. Say that again."

Barry furrowed his brow. "Say what?"

Fade rolled his eyes. "What you just said. About the records. Say it again. The only way..."

Barry gave his associates a hesitant glance. When no help came he sighed in resignation and acquiesced. "The only way anyone could know where these boys lived is if he's in the business or he got his hands on their records."

"Records. Records," Fade repeated, rolling his hand around in a beckoning motion before it came to him. "You mean... police records?"

"Yeah," Barry said with a shrug. "What else would I mean?"

Chapter 3
ON THE RECORD

"EXPLAIN TO ME—in *extensive* detail—why I should do anything to help you," Stern said while he cut off the ends of his cigar, letting the flakes of tobacco fall onto Fade's carpeting. "In fact, I think you should tell me why I bothered to trek halfway across town to be here."

"We need to check on the victims' police records, Captain. It's the first lead we've had since... Well, ever." Fade sat down at the edge of his desk, crossed his arms and frowned. "Besides, I thought the whole 'to catch a killer' idea was pretty self-explanatory. It's been in all the papers," he said as amiably as possible, though his patience was running thin. He hadn't had a full night's sleep in days and his nerves were beginning to fray.

"Mm," Stern sounded as he lit his cigar, blowing out a large cloud of yellow-grey smoke into the air. "Speaking of which," Stern said, fishing his jacket pocket. He pulled out a small piece of paper and carefully began unfolding it. "What was it you wrote about me in this week's *Planet*, again? I forget."

"Oh Lord," Fade grumbled, massaging his temples. He shot an aggravated look at Din, who simply shrugged in retaliation. "I should remind you that Din's my *ghostwriter*."

"Yes, but your name is still on the by-line," he replied, holding up the news clipping, his thumb curled around so it pointed directly at "by Foster Fade, Crime Spectacularist & Genius." He cleared his throat. "'Captain Stern, while perhaps working only under the purest of intentions, has done little to aid in the hunt for the Post Box Killer. His men have proven to be wholly unprepared and unequipped to face such a monster as the one currently stalking our streets. According to our sources, officials within the New York Police Department have called for the creation of a squad solely dedicated to this sort of special crime. "Until such time," said an officer on the condition anonymity, "I fear murderers such as the Post Box Killer will find a comfortable home within our city, and the price will be our very lives."' You know how much crap I got for that goddamn thing?" Stern angrily tossed the newspaper clipping at Fade, succeeding only in getting it to flutter harmlessly to the floor. He aimed an accusatory finger at Fade. "You wonder why we avoid you like the plague, it's 'cause of crap like that. It's bad enough the public is calling this madman a hero, you have to go and say I'm sleeping on the job."

Fade looked to his writer. "Din…" he pleaded.

She held up her hands and shook her head. "It was Gubb's idea, don't forget he is the publisher, like the Almighty, his word is law. Besides it's not my fault you boys in blue can't get your act together," she said to Stern before pointing to Fade, her cigarette smoldering between her fingers. "And it's *your* own damn fault that you don't read the articles before they go to print."

"I have a ghostwriter so I don't have to! Besides, I like reading the articles with the mugs! It's more… exciting that way."

"If you didn't want me to have *carte blanche*," Din shot back firmly, jutting her chin forward, "you shouldn't have given it!"

Fade gritted his teeth. "I'm usually kind of busy."

Din subtly raised her eyebrows as if she were trying to be impressed when there was a knock at the door. "Then get busy answering the door."

Fade sighed in frustration before shouting over his shoulder: "Come in!"

The boy from the mailroom risked his head into the office, his face a patchwork of red, maroon and crimson. "Uh, um… Mr. Fade?"

"What!" he snapped then thought better of it. "Sorry. Yes?"

"You've…" he said hesitantly before taking a long step in. He cleared his throat. "You've got a package, sir."

Fade's lips formed a white line at the sight of the small box in the boy's hand. A part of him felt as if he should be dismayed, but instead, he only felt numb. He walked around his desk and dropped into his chair. "Put it here," he said with an idle wave. "And *carefully*." He steepled his fingers and watched as the boy delicately placed the box on the desk and hurried away as fast as his scrawny legs could carry him.

Stern slowly took his cigar from his mouth and leaned forward. "Is that…?"

"What you think it is," Fade finished for him. "Yes. I'm afraid it is."

"Lucky number seven," Din said sardonically as she strolled over.

"Thank you for the commentary, Din."

"That's what I'm here for."

Stern extinguished his cigar angrily into Fade's ashtray. He pushed up his cap revealing for the first time the extent of the wine-stain birthmark, extending all the way from his eyebrow to the corner of his mouth.

"Congratulations, Captain. You finally get to experience the unwrapping of the murder weapon."

"Lucky me," Stern whispered.

Fade fed his finger under the brown paper wrapping and sliced sideways, tearing the tape free. He placed the discarded paper neatly to the side before pulling the cardboard box open.

Just as Fade expected, the note had a simple typewritten number seven above the guns model and make, a Browning Highpower M1935 9mm caliber. "'For all the ways that the laws of our city fail, Foster Fade acts as a counterbalance,'" he read the quote aloud. "'It can be argued that he protects the innocence of our citizens at the expense of his own.'" He massaged his eyes and took a long deep and quavering sigh. "Jesus Christ, this is from the first article."

Stern stepped over, wrapped his handkerchief around his hand, and picked the gun out of the box, delicately turning it over as if it were made of fine china when he suddenly blanched. "No," he gasped. "No, it can't be."

"Captain, what is it?"

"It's not possible."

Fade grabbed at Stern's wrist. "Captain."

Stern looked up from the gun and met Fade's gaze. "I know this gun." He tilted the gun toward Fade. "Right here, this skull and crossbones scratched into the handle. It's from the Sanderson Murders. Before your time. Nineteen Twenty-Eight or thereabout. This gun belonged to Austin Breslow, a hit man for the Murder Corporation, back before Nord took it over. They liked to call him Breslow Bones, partially because his face looked like Lon Chaney on a bad day, but mostly cause, well, he was a sick son of a bitch. He took the name to heart and started marking his guns with a skull and crossbones. Did it himself with a screwdriver, or so we heard. Maybe it was just to prove them right or maybe it just showed how crazy he is, one of the two. Anyway, we found the bodies, couple of young girls and this boy, Greg Sanderson, son of some mob boss, probably no older than seventeen, trussed up like turkeys on Thanksgiving. We knew it was Breslow; had it on some authority he was given the boy as a mark and the girls, well… wrong place, wrong time. Of course, there were others involved, Breslow's thugs, but we had Breslow. We arrested Breslow. We confiscated his guns, but then we could never link him to the murders, not conclusively enough for the courts. It was all circumstantial and hearsay so the trial went down the drain and Breslow went back out into the world."

Fade eyed the skull and bones carved into the gun. "Could this just be another one of Breslow's guns?"

Stern shook his head. "On my life, this is the same gun."

"Well," Fade sighed, "now, we know who our next victim is… Or *was*, for that matter."

"We can't know that for certain."

Fade firmed his lips. "No, Captain I think we can…"

Chapter 4
NO EVIDENCE

THE EVIDENCE ROOM sat in the bowels of the police department, a massive, vaguely organized closet stacked high with boxes, folders and files. Having struggled through New York City traffic, Fade, Din and Stern arrived there later than they hoped, with the sun a narrow sliver on the horizon. Sergeant Scott Tipton met them by the elevator, his uniform smartly pressed, hat tucked beneath his arm.

"Mr. Tipton, thank you for your time," Fade said cordially, though his gaze was focused the small sign above the entrance: "Authorized Personnel Only."

"That's Sergeant Tipton, but you can call me Scott, if you prefer, Mr. Fade," Tipton said with a firm shake. "Captain Stern tells me we might be of some assistance. Seems like you've got some things that might belong here."

"I sure hope so, Scott." Fade glanced back at Din, scribbling in her notebook. She looked up briefly and met his eyes, giving him a small nod. Din might not have been the investigator he was, but she knew the game was starting to get interesting.

"My wife's been a fan of your column since the first," Tipton was saying as he led them into the evidence room. "Reads it everyday like it's the King James. I read an article or two here and there, but me? I listen to the radio."

"Well, I appreciate that, Scott," Fade said, distracted as he looked over the room. "I'm always eager to hear about my fans. If you have something, I'd be happy to sign it for your wife. Just let me know her name."

Tipton smiled. "That's awfully kind of you, Mr. Fade, but you're not here to help me get brownie points with my old lady. Come; let's see if we can make it into print. Woodward, Lee!" he called out.

Two narrowly built clerks appeared out from the maze of boxes and shelves.

"Yes, sir?" asked Woodward, the taller of the two, a young man with rapidly thinning hair. He pulled off his green eyeshade and wiped his brow with the back of his sleeve.

"Can you two show Mr. Fade and Captain Stern around? Help them find whatever it is they're—"

"We're looking for box one-twenty-four," Stern interjected.

Woodward stood up stock straight at the request, as if he had been suddenly told to stand at attention. "The Sanderson Murders, Sir?"

Stern gave him a slow, sure nod. His eyes dropped to the floor before looking up at Fade. "The Sanderson Murders were my Waterloo, not about to forget a thing like that." He held Fade's gaze and for the first time they understood one another.

Woodward cleared his throat, beads of sweat forming on his brow. "So, what is it you're looking for?" he asked.

"Guns," Fade replied.

"More specifically, the absence thereof," Din added while she jotted down every note she could.

"Mm," Woodward sounded, rubbing his chin. He pulled a folder off a shelf and handed it to Fade. "This has everything on that aisle, all itemized, listed by box number and what's in it." He pointed over to a narrow walkway to his left. "If it was ever in here, it'll be listed there."

Fade skimmed through the folder until he came to the page listing box number one-twenty-four. He read down the list of items and suddenly felt lightheaded, as though someone had walked over his grave. He found the Browning 9mm listed, even with a description of the skull and crossbones etched into the handle. But there were other guns listed alongside some familiar names: Brandon McMillan, Michael Capitelli, Kevin Howard, Matthew Weglian, David Guida, and Alfonso Brown… All victims of the Post Box Killer. Only four suspects in box one-twenty-four were presumably still alive: Austin Breslow, Jonathan Pomatto, Pete Barry, and James Nord… He looked to Stern and Din then turned to the other clerk, Lee, who was shuffling behind them, his hand stuffed into his pockets. "Tell me, Mr. Lee, who else handles the evidence before it comes here?" Fade asked already knowing the answer.

Lee's eyes dropped to the ground, his face flush.

"We get most evidence here directly from the investigating officers," Sergeant Tipton answered for him. "Hold onto them until the trials—if there is one, you never know these days. Little kids getting shot down while they climb off a boat… no one catching the killers." He *tsked* in disappointment. "Things like that. If no trial comes, or if it falls through, we keep it all here just in case. You never know when a cold case might get warm." He leaned over and whispered to Fade: "And don't mind, ol' Anthony, he's one of your biggest fans; clips out your article as if he's starting a scrapbook. Makes my wife look like she's never even read one. He's just nervous, is all."

Fade gave Anthony a sidelong glance. "Huh. That so?"

"You know those clubs you mail away for in the funny books?" Woodward suggested. "You should start one up for yourself, you'll probably rake in the dough with guys like Anth."

"Very good idea, Mr. Woodward. Din? Make a note of that. Gubb will eat that up in a second. The man loves money, making it and spending it. An idea like that, Mr. Woodward, calls to both his demons." Fade caught Din subtly twirling her finger around in a circle and put himself back on course. "But we're moving away from why we're here: box one-twenty-four."

Woodward nodded. "I'll get right on it," he said, dashing down an aisle.

"Scott, how many clerks work down here?" Fade asked.

Tipton counted in his head. "About five, maybe six. We work in rotations for the most part, so I only see about two or three of them at a time."

"Thank you," Fade said. "Excuse us a moment." He beckoned Din as he pulled Stern over to the side.

"Don't tell me you're thinking it's one of my officers," Stern whispered firmly to Fade, his lips snarling. "That's crossing the line."

"The line's been crossed, Captain," Fade replied sharply, careful not to raise his voice. "We didn't do the crossing, but we're already far on the other side. If the guns were taken from here, it stands to reason that someone who works here must be behind the murders."

Stern shook his head in disbelief. "That's impossible… You can't tell me—"

"Captain…" Fade said softly, placing a conciliatory hand on Stern's shoulder. "I really don't see a way around it…"

"My gut tells me Woodward," Din said. "The way he acted when you asked for box one-twenty-four… I'm no 'Crime Spectacularist,' but I know a guilty conscience when I see one."

"What about Lee?" Fade asked with a slight nod toward the diminutive clerk. "Even Tipton said he clips out my articles and our killer—"

"We're jumping at shadows," Stern snapped. "Might as well say Tipton or Tipton's wife are the killers. Just because someone works here or happens to be a fan of yours doesn't make the—"

"This about the Post Box Killer?" Lee asked meekly, speaking up for the first time, nervously lacing and unlacing his fingers.

Fade turned to consider Lee. "Perhaps."

The tip of Lee's tongue mollusked out from the corner of his mouth and ran hesitantly along his top lip. "Been reading lot about that. People been calling him a hero, killing gangsters and all, kinda like how you capture them, but a bit more final, y'know? How many has it been now? Seven? Eight?"

"Seven," Fade said, slowly walking toward Lee. Despite his placid expression, Fade's heart was going mad in his chest, jostling around like a soda bottle ready to burst.

Lee's eyebrows raised in surprise. "That so!"

"But then again, the seventh gun only just came in today. Now, tell me, Mr. Lee," he calmly said, towering over the clerk, "because I am curious—quite curious—as to how you would know that…"

Lee shrugged and stammered. "I—I dunno. Just guessed."

"Fade…" Stern tried to interject. He placed a hand on Fade's narrow arm. "Maybe you should step back."

Fade raised an eyebrow, ignoring Stern. "'Just guessed?'"

"I suppose," the clerk whispered nervously, his eyes fluttering. "I mean… guy like that pr—probably won't stop on his own, not unless you—"

"Sir!" Woodward suddenly shouted, his feet pounding against the floor as he raced toward them, his face white.

Fade felt his fingers tremble and his jaw tighten up when he saw Woodward's pale expression.

"What is it, Woodward?" Sergeant Tipton asked sharply. "Where's box one-twenty-four?"

Woodward shook his head in disbelief. "That's the thing, sir… It's empty."

Chapter 5
MASKS

BRESLOW'S BODY WAS found in a park two blocks away from his home, a 9mm bullet lodged in the back of his head. Stern and Fade discovered the body themselves, placed under a tree like a present on Christmas morning. Stern was stone-faced throughout; watching quietly as the body was photographed, bagged, and shipped off to the morgue. It wasn't until the car ride back to the *Planet* that he spoke up.

"That was *my* case," he growled through his teeth. "Breslow was mine, I was supposed to be the one—" His voice choked for a moment before he composed himself. He slammed his hand against the wheel. "He's not making it better, you understand?! I don't care if the people think he's a hero, he's *not* making it better."

Fade looked out the window as the lights of the city strolled by. "I know, Captain, believe me, I know."

"If we could only have taken him then."

"We need to catch him in the act. You know that better than I, Captain. Without that, we have no proof."

Stern sucked at his teeth. "I want you to promise me something; you listening, Fade? You need to promise me that if this thing works, he's mine. You get me. I'm the one taking him in. Write want you want in the papers, I don't give a rat's ass what it says, so long as I'm the one throwing the cuffs on that weasel's puny wrists and the city *knows* that we will not let vigilantes—That vigilantes will not be suffered. Not anymore."

Fade glanced over at Stern, the wine stain redder than ever. "Promise."

"ALL RIGHT, MY money's on Lee," Din said awhile later, watching Fade furiously pace his lab in the back of his office. He had laid out his plan to her, what little of it there was, though to call it a plan was generous at best. A "favor" was perhaps more apt.

"Sorry, but you already made your bet," Fade replied halfheartedly, throwing a thick, heavy garment next to an assortment of gadgets on the central worktable. "Can't change it now."

Din measured him for a moment, taking a thoughtful puff of her cigarette as the gadgets piled up. "You sure this is going to work?"

"Sure," he said with a nonchalant shrug as he examined a small microphone the size of his thumb, recalling the next name on the list below Breslow's.

Din cocked a suspicious eyebrow. She tapped the end of her cigarette into the ashtray. "I'm going on record that this *isn't* the stupidest idea you've ever had."

"Thank you."

"But you've had better."

"As long as I've had worse," he paused to lean over the worktable, looking over his small mountain of machines. He picked up one that looked like a spring-loaded wrist brace. "But if you have a better idea, I'd love to hear it."

Din let out a sardonic laugh. "Naw, you do the heroing. I'll stick with the printed word. Helluva lot safer."

"The pen is mightier than the sword," Fade retorted, strapping on the wrist brace.

"Too bad we're dealing with guns."

THE MAN CLOSED his eyes in ecstasy and let out a long quivering breath. Sweat had begun to form at his brow and his hand dug deeper into his pocket, his fingers fiddling with his piece. It wasn't his weapon, not really, but for the time being, while he was fulfilling his mission—the one He had given him—it would be his to carry. And to have met Him, to have stood so close to Him, to know they had shared the same air; it made the man feel alive, invulnerable.

He watched his target move behind the windows, a tall tower of a silhouette. The list had named him Jonathan Pomatto, known by his compatriots as "Wits," perhaps because he had too many or too few, the man didn't care. He was a criminal, a parasite leeching off the city, a roach ready to be crushed, killed by his own gun.

The light switched off in Pomatto's apartment and the man instinctually cocked back the hammer of the old fashioned Colt Military Model 1902, confiscated during a raid back in twenty-nine, when the cops had more gumption than they did now. Apparently, Pomatto had been something of a war hero before he went sour and turned to a life of crime. Despicable, the man thought, spitting a yellow wad of phlegm to the ground. To serve one's country and then debase all it stood for. Pomatto deserved this. They all deserved this.

Overhead, clouds blanketed the sky. It would rain soon and empty the streets. The man smiled.

He moved toward the side of the steps and discreetly adjusted his pants, suddenly feeling exposed. This part always confused and mortified him. He wasn't supposed to feel this way, he was sure of it, but as with the others, he was stiff as a board, excited and shivering.

He lowered his hat and adjusted the scarf resting beneath his nose. His suit, overcoat, fedora and scarf were all black as midnight, making him look nothing more than a shadow, a spider on the wall. He needed his identity to remain a secret. It was protection, a way to ensure the mission could continue as long as possible.

The door opened and Pomatto strolled down the steps, tugging the front of his fedora down over his eyes. He paused at the bottom of the steps to button his coat around his narrow frame and headed down the street. The man let out a long quavering sigh as Pomatto walked past. The man smiled. He pulled out his gun and followed after his target, careful not to get too close until the right moment.

Pomatto turned right at the corner, his long legs moving him faster than the man could have anticipated. The man broke into a jog, struggling to keep up. His breath was growing short—he wasn't as young as he used to be—and found he was humming despite himself, like this was all some kind of game. But then again, wasn't it? The stakes were larger of course, so *important*, but it was a game nonetheless. Cops and robbers, heroes and villains. He waited until Pomatto rounded another corner and cut through an alleyway before he allowed himself to catch up with his prey.

Now, that dark little voice said. It was time and the man listened.

He raced forward and pressed Pomatto's own gun against the crook of his back.

"Johnny 'Wits' Pomatto," he whispered excitedly. He was so *tall*, he realized. He might have to shoot him in the spine; his head was so far away. "I know your crimes and you are guilty. Guilty of theft, of racketeering, of bootlegging, of violence, of *murder*. You are guilty and you will have your judgment."

Pomatto instinctually held up his arms. "Who are you?"

The man sniggered. "Names, names, names. They gave me a name in the paper, first, middle and last. But that's not my name, not really. It's just an alias, a way to protect me so I may complete my mission. Now get down to your knees."

"Mission?" Pomatto said curiously, as though there was no fear in his heart. "Is that what you call it?"

"Don't question me, worm," the Post Box Killer barked. "Get down to your knees!"

But Pomatto simply laughed, a proud, powerful laugh.

"You… You don't get to laugh!" he shouted shoving the gun hard into Pomatto's back. "Do you know *who* I am?!"

"Go ahead and fire, won't do you much good, I'm covered head to toe in lead lined protection. It's my own design. Snazzy stuff, really. Weighs a ton, but then again, we're all the victims of fashion aren't we?"

"What—I—You…" the Killer stammered.

"And even if you *did* kill me—which you won't—it wouldn't do you much good. There are cops surrounding the whole place, and probably a bit further beyond that. The whole place is staked out; we've been watching you this whole time. I'm sure Din's transcribing everything we say, I've got this neat little wireless microphone hooked up to my lapel. Her headphones sit inside her ears. Like I said, snazzy stuff."

"But… but… how?"

"Box number one-twenty-four," Pomatto said as he slowly turned around.

The Killer's eyes went wide and almost fell over in shock. "You're… you're not…" he stammered, the gun shaking in his hands as he fell back a step. "You're *Him*!"

"Yup," Foster Fade said with a grim smile. A small pistol ejected from the inside of his sleeve into his hand. He pressed the barrel into the Post Box Killer's chest. "One of the benefits of knowing a near seven-foot tall gangster is you can fit into his clothing. Now, who are you?"

The Post Box Killer smiled and tugged at his scarf. "Oh, you know quite well, Mr. Fade."

Fade squinted, unable to ignore the trepidation forming in his chest. Though the scarf only covered the lower half of the Killer's face, he could tell without a doubt that it wasn't Anthony Lee standing before him.

The Killer let out a soft, nervous laugh as he slowly shook his head. "Good. So good." He flipped the gun around in his hand and struck Fade in the jaw. The blow was enough to knock Fade back, but only just; the Killer had pulled his punch. Fade's hat flew from his head, his finger squeezed down on the trigger and the bullet went wild. The Killer spun around on his heel and raced out of the alleyway into the streets.

Stern and the other officers ran out from the shadows, their pistols already drawn. "You! Stay here in case he doubles back. You two! Get a squad car and see if you can cut him off."

"Hell," Fade cursed, holding his jaw. "Was not expecting that."

"You were supposed to hold onto him!" Stern shouted, grabbing at Fade's sleeve.

"He socked me in the jaw!" Fade snapped back as they ran into the street, dodging an angry flurry of cars.

"So? I've been wanting to do that for months."

"He's a strong little bugger." Fade commented, as the Post Box Killer ducked into an alleyway across the street.

"Everyone's little to you. Come on, you're with me."

"Partners in crime, eh?" Fade said with a crooked grin.

"Shut up."

Stern and Fade ran up to the edge of the alleyway and pinned themselves against either wall. There was a trickle of rain pattering against the pavement with a discordant rhythm as the clouds decided to open themselves up to the world.

"How many bullets you have left in that pop gun?" Stern asked, gesturing with his chin.

"Well," Fade said thoughtfully as he unhooked the gun from his wrist. "Considering it's only big enough to carry one…"

Stern rolled his eyes. "Fantastic."

"But not to worry." Fade dropped the gun to the ground. "I brought a spare," he said, drawing a massive double-barreled gun from his side holster as a rejoinder.

Stern gave the half-pistol, half-shotgun a suspicious look. "Maybe letting you come armed wasn't such a great idea."

Fade smiled. "It's my own design."

Stern rolled his eyes. “Well, la-dee-da. Listen up, Mr. Post Box, you’re surrounded!” he shouted into the alleyway. “You might try to run, you might even try using the fire escapes to get up to the roof, but it won’t do you any good. No matter how fast you can run we’ll catch you. So, you might want to drop Mr. Pomatto’s gun, put up your hands and get ready for the end of your little bout of celebrity. You don’t... Well, let’s just say there’s a bit more than seven guns aimed your way. How’s that sound?”

“Sounds like an interesting proposition, Captain,” the Post Box Killer called back after a moment, his singsong voice bouncing around the alleyway. “Why don’t you come in here and discuss it?”

“Drop the gun and I will.”

Several moments passed before the clatter of metal against pavement. “There you are, Captain,” the Killer shouted.

Stern glanced over, his face matching his name, and gave Fade a subtle nod.

“All yours,” Fade said, living up to his promise.

A grim smile curled on Stern’s lips. He held up a hand, telling Fade to stay put. He rounded the corner, his sidearm raised, and stepped into the alleyway when there was a sudden crack of gunfire. He fell to the ground without so much as a grunt of pain. His head rolled to the side, his eyes staring up at Fade as if waiting for a response that would never come. A coldness settled over Fade and the gun in his hand suddenly felt ready to explode. All it needed was a target.

“Just you and me now, Mr. Fade,” the Post Box Killer called. “Well, us and everyone else watching. But that’s how it always was, wasn’t it?”

Fade grimaced, unable to look away from Stern’s dead eyes. A pool of blood had begun to form beneath the police captain’s body, glistening black in the night. “What makes you think I’m that stupid?” he shouted back without emotion.

“Never said you were Mr. Fade. In fact, I think quite the opposite.”

“And how do I know you won’t shoot me the moment I walk in?” The other officers were moving in closer, waiting for the right time to strike. But that wasn’t the story, not the one that would make it to print. This was Fade’s story, had been since the very beginning.

“By your own admission, you have bulletproof protection.”

“Maybe I was just lying so you wouldn’t shoot me.”

“Come now, Mr. Fade, you would never lie to *me*.”

Fade chewed the inside of his cheek, disturbed by the Killer’s tone.

It wasn't threatening or goading, it was… benevolent, as if they were old friends reuniting after years apart. Fade closed his eyes and took a deep breath. The lead-lined suit should work, in theory, but he had never had the chance to properly test it; nor did it cover his head. One clean shot and his photo would run alongside his obituary on the front page. He ran his free hand through his long hair and adjusted his tie. Well, if he was going to die, he might as well look good.

"All right, I'm here," Fade called out as he stepped, cocking back both hammers of his gun.

The Post Box Killer nonchalantly strolled out of the shadows, his arms raised, hands empty. A small piece of scrap metal lay between them, the Killer's bluff. Fade raised his gun and aimed for the Killer's head.

"Are you going to kill me, Mr. Fade?" he asked evenly, as if they were discussing game results.

"Not really my style. I'm more the catch and carry sort," Fade admitted, fighting back the urge to fire. It was only then that he noticed that Pomatto's gun was missing. "Let the law sort out the rest."

The Killer chuckled. "Come now, Mr. Fade, we both know the law doesn't work. It's why we're here!"

"Where's Pomatto's gun?" Fade asked, taking a half step back as the Killer approached.

"Ah, how careless of me," the Killer slowly reached into his pocket, pulled out the pistol and dropped it to the ground. "I haven't drilled it yet like I did the others. I usually wait until I get home. Very powerful, cost quite a bit. But I'm sure the bullet in Captain Stern will match the weapon nicely."

There was no denying the man was insane, but to offhandedly confess to not one, but eight murders took a special kind of crazy. "Move and I'll fire, you understand?" Fade said aloud. "This thing packs quite a punch so there wouldn't be a lot of you left to scrape off the floor."

The Killer gave him a slow nod, the corners of his thin smile peaked out from beneath the scarf, sending shivers down Fade's spine. He walked over to Pomatto's gun and kicked it away; careful to never let his eyes, or his gun, off the Killer, who simply watched Fade with an eerie sense of awe. Fade stepped over and knocked the Killer's black fedora off with the end of his double-barreled gun.

"Close your damn eyes," Fade commanded and the Killer instantly complied, the smile threatening to rip his face in half. Fade reached over to pull off the scarf when he hesitated, suddenly feeling as if he hadn't showered in weeks. His fingers unconsciously curled inward, but Fade forced himself forward and ripped the scarf off the Killer's face.

Fade's mouth open and closed in shock, tears welling up in his eyes from anger and shock.

"Tipton?" he whispered.

"Good job, sir," Sergeant Scott Tipton said with a watermelon grin. "Damn good job."

Chapter 6
THE MISSION

FADE AND DIN sat silently in the hallway facing one another, though their eyes drilled through the floor. Fade leaned his elbows heavily on his knees, his clothes still soaked from the rain, his long hair dripping onto his collar. Din was bone dry, her chromium hair glowing in the warm incandesce of the police department lights. A cigarette smoldered between her fingers, untouched since she lit it. They had yet to speak a word to one another, unsure what they would say even if they did.

"Sir?" a voice growled through the haze a minute, an hour, a day later.

Fade glanced up to find a scruffy looking lieutenant standing over him. He recognized the face but couldn't place the name.

"Any word?" Fade asked, his own voice hollow to his ears.

The lieutenant shook his head. "No good ones at least."

"Dammit." Fade put his head in his hands. Stern had never been a friend, but he was still an ally. "Don't even know if he had a family."

"Two daughters," the lieutenant replied. "Six and eight. But that's... That's not why I'm here."

Fade looked back up at the lieutenant.

"He's asking—" the lieutenant cleared his throat. "He's asking to see you, sir."

"Why?"

The lieutenant shook his head. "Not my place to ask what crazy wants."

Fade stood up from his chair, an effort that felt like it took millennia to achieve. He tugged at the bottom his suit jacket and smoothed out the wrinkles of his tie before he gave the lieutenant a terse nod and began following him down the hallway.

"What're you going to say to him, Foster?" Din called after him.

Fade paused and shook his head.

"Those were my words too, you know," she said mournfully. "Those were my words too."

Fade met her gaze and frowned, understanding all too well.

A BARE BULB sent a harsh cone of illumination over the table in the center of the room, the walls hidden in darkness. There was a vacant seat across from Tipton; the leather cushions worn down, thick black hairs sticking out at the edges. Tipton's hands were shackled to his chair while his eyes followed Fade like a child watching a firefly.

"Hello, Mr. Fade," Tipton said warmly as Fade sat down. "Thank you for coming to see me."

"You know me," Fade replied. "I'm always eager to meet my fans. If I had known earlier I definitely would have signed something for you."

Tipton leaned his head slightly forward. "We did have a bit of fun, didn't we?"

"We did," Fade said, expressionless.

"It took some planning, of course. Rome wasn't built in a day."

Fade nodded. "Of course."

"It was a godsend when I found the box," Tipton began excitedly. "Like it had been left there just for me to find, filled with the guns of *guilty* men, men who had escaped the law. I found it and I knew what I had to do. 'For all the ways that the laws of our city fail, Foster Fade acts as a counterbalance… He protects the innocence of our citizens at the expense of his own.' I understood," he said as if quoting scripture. "I took the guns home one by one, it isn't easy to steal from the police, you must understand. And then of course, I had to track down these… these… *vile* men," he said through gritted teeth, spittle flecking his lips, his eyes going wide. "I had to find them and wait. So many nights. Waiting. Watching. And when I had them alone, I followed them, chased them down and told them of their crimes. I let them know what they had done to this city, to *our* city. I told them of our *judgment*, their *sentence*. I killed them with their own guns so they knew, so that they *understood*."

"And then you drilled out the guns."

"To keep the mission going," Tipton added matter-of-factly, "for as long as we could. I was able to retrieve most of the bullets—the ones that went through the skulls—but I knew if they found the bullets they would be able to match the bullets to the guns so I had to be careful. You wrote about that in your twenty-eighth article, how guns leave fingerprints. So I drilled."

Fade's teeth began to chatter. "Then why did you send them to me?"

Tipton's eyes blinking rapidly as he considered Fade, bemused. "Why—Why wouldn't I?"

Gooseflesh covered Fade's neck. His gaze briefly dropped to his hands as he tried to process what Tipton was telling him. There was so much dirt caked beneath his fingernails, how had they gotten so filthy?

Tipton took a long, deep satisfactory breath, his eyes watering. "I'm very proud of you. So very proud."

Fade met Tipton's gaze. "Excuse me?" he said, feeling as if his head was in a fog.

Tipton leaned forward. "I knew you'd be the one to catch me," he said, a father proud of his son. "Never a doubt in my mind."

"You..." Fade shifted uncomfortably in his chair. "You *wanted* to be caught?"

"Oh, of course, Mr. Fade," Tipton said. "I'm a monster. You said so yourself. But it couldn't be just anyone. No, no, no. Stern wasn't worthy. It *had* to be you," he said, pointing a finger at Fade.

Fade ran a hand over his cheek, finding it grizzled. When was the last time he had shaven? Last week? Two weeks ago? How long had this been going on, how long since the first gun?

"What about your wife?" he heard himself ask.

Tipton's lip snarled and he looked away. "Worthless harlot." he spat under his breath. "Worthless, worthless, *whore*."

He licked his lips, his throat painfully dry. "Mr. Tipton—"

"I told you, Mr. Fade. It's Scott."

"Mister Tipton," Fade said pointedly. "I need you to explain to me why."

Tipton's eyes fluttered. "I... I don't understand, Mr. Fade..."

"Why have you been taunting me?!" Fade shouted, slamming his hands down on the table. "The guns, the quotes! To what end, dammit! What were you trying to prove?!"

Tipton's lips pursed and flattened, his fingernails tapped against the metal of his chair. "You know why I did this. I was doing what you told me to do. 'Fade faces criminals head on and never looks back, not for himself, but for all of us, because this is as much Fade's battle as it is our own.' That was in your first article, Mr. Fade. You told me to. I did it for you," he said, pleasantly. "I did this all for you."

Fade jumped out of his chair and rushed to the door, suddenly feeling dizzy, as if he was suffocating and the walls inching closer. He put his hand on the doorknob and hesitated. "You misunderstood, Mr. Tipton," he managed, his voice shaking. "This was never a *mission*, never a calling. It's a job, simple as that. Entertainment for the masses."

Tipton shook his head slowly and smiled. "This was all for you, Mr. Fade. All for you."

Fade fled out of the room, slamming the door behind him. It was all he could do not to scream. He wanted to fall to his hands and knees, to break down into tears, but the mugs were watching and the show as still going on. So he kept his eyes on the floor, his fists clenched and let the mugs see the man they wanted to see.

A pair of red stilettos appeared under his nose. "You're a terrible liar, Foster," Din said, tilting up his face by his chin.

"Am I?" Fade croaked with a hollow smile.

She tapped the headphone tucked in her ear and the small microphone on his lapel; he had forgotten to turn it off. "You might be able to fool yourself that this is all just a job for you, a way to pay the bills and sit in the spotlight." She took a drag of her cigarette and looked him in the eye. "But I know you better than that."

"Do you now?" he said, fixing his tie.

Din nodded, exhaling a cloud of smoke. "It's a lie I tell myself. It makes it easier, because what kind of person would do what we do if it wasn't for the money?" Din let the question hang unanswered between them. "But don't worry, your secret is safe with me."

Fade coyly raised an eyebrow. "And which is secret that?"

Din gave him a somber smile. "All of them. Come on, there's a bunch of mobsters dressed up like Indians robbing the First National. If that's not the most ridiculous thing I've ever said I don't know what is."

Fade managed a chuckle. "Well, then. Geronimo."

THE END

DERRICK FERGUSON

THE CIDER KING MURDER

AN ADVENTURE OF FOSTER FADE
THE CRIME SPECTACULARIST

"SO WHAT DO you think?"

"What do I think of what?"

"Of this, nitwit."

"What exactly is *this* and what does it have to do with me?"

The speaker was a tall gangly man with colorless eyes and hair to match. Lean and lanky, Foster Fade looked as if he could have easily benefitted from another fifty pounds of weight on him. His Dunston Brothers three piece suit had to have cost at least five hundred bucks but looked as if he'd slept in it the night before. Which he most likely had. The tie around his neck hung loosely and the top button undone. His large, bony hands were thrust into his pants pockets as he looked around and scowled.

The *this* he referred to was the brand new radio station recently built on the completely renovated thirty-ninth floor of the *Planet* Tower. The auditorium, meant for an audience of two hundred, was filled with brand spanking new seats. Over to the far left of the auditorium sat the studio itself complete with control room and a long soundproof window. Foster Fade's disparaging gaze swiveled from the seats to the stage.

Dinamenta Stevens placed red-nailed hands on her wonderfully rounded hips. "This is where you're going to be broadcasting from, naturally."

"Broadcasting what, exactly?"

"*The Planet*'s first radio show, natch. Broadcast from here three times a week, the Adventures of The Crime Spectacularist! Live from the roof of *The Planet* itself, The Crime Spectacularist will astound America as he narrates in his own words how he solves the most baffling of cases and brings to justice the criminal masterminds that plague our society!"

Fade pulled out a pack of Beemans gum. He unwrapped a stick, popped it into his wide mouth and chewed with all the manners and grace of a plow mule. He gave the auditorium one last look before turning to Din, his hands back in his pockets. "Nuts."

"What?"

"I said nuts and nuts is what I mean. The deal was that I solve crimes and you write the stories. I make with the gadgets, you handle the snappy prose. I don't do radio." Fade turned and walked out of the auditorium. Din followed him into the wide corridor, her stiletto heels click-clacking on the genuine Barkley marble floor.

"You can't do this, Fade! Hackrox paid a bundle for that studio! And he built it because I sold him on the idea of a radio show about you!"

Fade stopped at the elevator and one unusually long finger stabbed at the UP button. "Then it would have behooved you to have talked to me first. I don't perform for anybody, Din."

"But this is for money!"

"I got money."

"A lot of money!"

"I have a lot of money. You do, too. Last I heard the only person on the *Planet* staff who makes more than you is Hackrox himself and he owns the paper."

The elevator door opened smoothly and the operator within nodded and smiled at Fade as he and Din stepped inside. The car contained eight or nine other passengers, some of who gaped at Fade in amazement. They plainly recognized him from his many pictures in *The Planet* on practically a daily basis. All the operators knew Fade and he knew them, as well he should. They were a valuable part of his operation, keeping their eyes on everybody who went in and out of the Planet tower. "My floor," Fade said simply. The operator nodded, closed the door and the elevator smoothly headed up to the fortieth floor.

"Hey, I need to go down! I'll be late for work!" some wag in the rear of the car yelped.

"I'll be glad to take you down to your floor, sir. Once I've taken Mr. Fade to his floor."

"Are you really The Crime Spectacularist?" The bejeweled dowager asking the question seemed overcome with surprise at being so close to Fade. It was hard to tell if she were actually furiously blushing with excitement through all the rouge on her wrinkled cheeks.

"I am, madam." Fade bent down and kissed her left cheek. "And now you are the envy of your garden club for at your next meeting you can regale them with the tale of how you were kissed by The Crime Spectacularist himself."

The elevator door opened and Fade walked toward the door leading to his suite of offices, eating up the distance with his long-legged stride.

Din was right behind him, her heels striking the marble sounding like a series of very sharp air-gun shots.

"So exactly what is Hackrox supposed to do with a brand new broadcast studio and auditorium?" Din demanded haughtily.

"Tell him to hire King Mantell and his orchestra. I like King's music." Fade unlocked the door to his suite of offices, which included the reception room, the main office and his lab. Adjoining the offices were his private living quarters: the master bedroom and bath, the kitchen and dining area and a guest bedroom used most frequently by Din when they were working on a case. Which they usually were. In fact, it was rare when they weren't working on a case. But nothing had come up in the past week and so left to their devices, Fade and Din did what they usually did when they were bored: they barked and bit at each other.

"One of these days I got to hire me a secretary," Fade muttered as he continued on through the reception area to his office. He threw himself down on the couch and folded his big hands across his chest. "Office should have a secretary. It looks too bare outside there."

The phone on Fade's desk rang. "You wouldn't know what to do with a secretary if you had one," Din replied as she picked it up. "Foster Fade's office…oh, hey O'Toole, how's tricks?" Din fell silent as she listened to the voice on the other end. "Really? That's swell! Thanks, O'Toole! You can collect your fifty at the end of the week." Din hung up the phone. "C'mon, get cracking, genius."

Fade lazily opened one eye. "What's got your motor running?"

"Murder!"

Fade yawned. "Not interested."

"You better get interested, buster! We haven't had a juicy case all week and when Hackrox hears how you've blown off the radio show idea, he's not going to be a happy camper! They best thing you can be doing is working on getting me some fresh ink for the evening edition."

Fade swung his long legs off the couch. "You may have a point there. What's this murder that's got you all atwitter?"

"You heard of Philip Williams?"

"Sure. The Cider King. If you drink cider anywhere on the east coast, you're drinking Williams Cider. He's been murdered?"

"He's dead at any rate. But you're going to prove it was murder."

"Who called you?"

"Patrolman O'Toole. I've got fifty cops on my payroll. Anytime they call me and tip me off to a murder, it's fifty bucks in their kick."

"Corrupting honest officers of the law. How low can you go?"

"How low you want me to go? C'mon, get up and let's ankle it!"

"Waitaminnit. You said that Williams is dead but that I have to prove it was murder? What do the cops think?"

"It doesn't matter what they think!" Din cried in exasperation, reaching down to seize Fade by the lapels of his suit jacket and yanking him to his feet. An impressive feat of desperation that, considering that on his feet, the top of Din's head stopped somewhere around the base of Fade's breastbone, so tall was he. "You're going to prove it was murder!"

FADE'S FIRE ENGINE red Packard convertible came to a crunching halt at the gates of the Williams estate. Four uniformed cops guarded those gates and one ambled over to the vehicle. The cop touched two fingers to the brim of his cap. "Hiya, Din!"

"This here's O'Toole," Din said to Fade by way of explanation. "You can get us in, O'Toole?"

"For fifty bucks I'd get you into The Vatican if'n I hadta. Just do me a favor and tell Detective Heath you showed me phony I.D., okay?"

Din smiled, nodded and O'Toole shouted for the other three cops to open the gates. Shortly, the Packard was through and Fade continued driving to the immense two story country style house. Fade parked in front and they climbed out. "Grab that bag for me, willya?" Fade asked.

"Grab it yourself. I'm a reporter, not a pack mule."

Fade sighed and left the bag there. It contained a selection of forensic equipment that he would normally carry with him to the scene of a murder but then again, he wasn't even sure this was a murder yet. He unwrapped another stick of gum and popped it into his mouth.

They went on inside to encounter what looked like the city's entire police force occupying the entrance hall of the mansion. "Didn't know they were holding the policeman's ball here this year," Fade muttered.

"Fade! What the hell you doing here? How'd you catch the squeal on this?" Barrel-chested Detective Don Heath shoved his way through the crowd of uniformed cops toward Fade and Din.

"Good morning to you too, Detective. Who's protecting the city while you're all in here?"

"Don't crack wise with me, Fade! I wanna know how you heard

about this!"

Fade jerked a thumb over his shoulder at Din. "Ask her. But do me a favor, okay? Don't get her confused with a pack mule."

Detective Heath whirled on Din. "Okay, sister! Spill! Who tipped you off? If it was one of my boys I'll have his badge before lunchtime!"

"I'm a reporter, Heath. Which means I got a nose for news." Din tapped her cute snub of a nose. "And this is telling me that you're as nervous as a long tailed cat in a room full of rocking chairs."

"That's because I got one of the city's fat cats lying dead in the next room and nobody can tell me how he died!"

"Well, that's what I brought The Crime Spectacularist here for, Detective."

"I got my own people, thank you very much. Last thing I need is Fade—" Heath broke off suddenly and looked around. "Hey, where is Fade, anyway?" Heath stomped off in the direction of the library. Din followed.

Fade stood in the doorway of the library, chewing his gum with the gusto of a horse chewing a raw carrot. He extended an arm that looked twice as long as the average man's arm. Indeed, it was long enough to bar both Din and Detective Heath from entering the room. "Just stop right there."

"You've got a nerve! I'm in charge here!" Detective Heath snarled.

"Then you should have kept everybody out of this room who had no business being in there. Even from here I can see that at least ten different men have been stomping around in there like a herd of water buffalos. Valuable evidence has undoubtedly been destroyed."

"Photos were taken as well as fingerprints!"

Fade ignored Detective Heath. His colorless eyes roamed over the floor to ceiling bookshelves, the heavy Italian furniture, the tables next to the window. The body of Philip Williams lay on his back next to the inlaid sideboard bar. His final expression was one of complete and utter neutrality. As if he died with no emotion at all. Only after Fade had made a complete visual inspection of the room did he go in. Fade busied himself examining the bookcases first thing.

"I want the both of you out of here right now or so help me, I'll jug you for interference with a police investigation."

"Was it murder?" Din had her notepad out, already furiously taking notes and totally ignoring Heath's threats.

Heath sighed impatiently. Despite his bluff and bluster he well knew

Fade's capabilities. And this would be a high profile case that the press would be all over. Heath sighed again and gave in. "Okay. All we know is that the poor man died. His daughter came home from being away for a few days and found him here like that. Called us straightaway."

"This room was for show," Fade said, moving away from the bookcases, brushing his hands together. "Whoever does his housekeeping is lazier than a Kansas City pimp. There's dust on top of the books and in the space behind them."

"So?"

"Means that Mr. Williams didn't read. The books are here just to impress."

"I don't see what that has to do with anything. So the man didn't read. So what? I don't read either." Heath grunted.

Fade hunkered down next to the body. At the same time he rummaged inside his pockets of his suit jacket, looking for something. Fade knew he had it as he very rarely went anywhere without it. "In your case, you not reading is probably because you're too lazy to pick up a book and give your brain cells some proper exercise once in a while. In the case of our Mr. Williams, it indicates something else." From his inside jacket pocket Fade withdrew what looked to be an oversized pair of black horn-rimmed spectacles. Fade put these on and with his index finger, manipulated a small slide lever on the bridge. A slight whirring and clicking emanated from the glasses as he did so.

Intrigued despite himself, Detective Heath bent down to get a closer look and said, "Never seen specs like those before."

"Mechanical eyeglasses," Fade replied as he looked at the corpse's hands, neck and face. "There are different lenses in the frame and by switching back and forth they go from giving me microscopic accuracy when looking at things close up or telescopic to look at objects far away. Get outta my light, willya?"

"Where's the daughter now?" Din asked insistently. "And didn't Williams have a wife? Where is she now?"

Before Detective Heath could answer, a snarling voice interrupted. "Detective Heath, what the hell is Fade doing here?"

Fade looked up from his examination, the lenses in his mechanical eyeglasses clicking and whirring as they changed to accommodate his vision to focus on what he looked at now. Which was the angry face of Coroner Jarred Long. "I want Fade out of here, Detective. Right now."

"You can't do that!" Din shouted wrathfully, forcefully placing herself between Long and Heath. "Foster Fade is a staff member of *The Planet* and that means he has all the rights and protection of the press!"

"Fade's not a snoopy reporter like you. He's just a plain snoop who thinks he's better than the police."

"Smarter at any rate. Or don't you read *The Planet* daily?" Din snapped.

"I want him out, Heath, or I'm going to the commissioner. I won't have Fade second guessing me."

"Okay, Fade, you heard the man. You—" Heath turned around as he spoke. He stopped in mid-sentence as Fade was gone. At some point during their arguing, Fade had simply left the room. "Where'd he go?" Heath said, whirled back on Din. "Where'd he go?"

"Beats me, Detective. I was busy being chewed out by our favorite coroner here."

"As long as he's gone I don't much care where he is," Long grumbled. "Now if you can get this skirt outta here, maybe I can get some work done!"

"Have you examined the body yet? Was it murder?" Din asked.

"That's none of your business! Heath—"

"Quit your bellyaching. It's giving me a headache." Fade said as he reentered the library, holding onto the large satchel he had earlier asked Din to bring along. He'd pushed his mechanical eyeglasses back on top of his head. He walked over to the body, knelt and opened up the satchel.

"Get away from that body, Fade! Heath, are you just going to stand there and do nothing?"

"If he wants to solve this murder he will," Fade said quietly, rummaging around in the satchel. He withdrew several pieces of what looked like shiny typing paper. He selected one and pressed the corpse's entire open left hand to it, held it there firmly.

"What the devil do you think you're doing? Heath!"

"I could tell you but The Good Lord has allotted me only so much breath for this life and I'd rather not waste what I have trying to explain." Fade continued to hold the open hand to the paper as he looked up at Long. "Let me ask you a question, useless as it may be. Did you examine this body's hands?"

"Of course I did!"

"Didn't you notice the unusual scarring on said hands?"

"My husband was a working man all his life, sir. He was proud of those scars as it showed the world he wasn't afraid to get his hands dirty."

Emma Williams stood in the doorway of the library, hands folded together, standing ramrod straight and letting her eyes rest briefly on everybody in the room before she stepped in and continued. "My husband's hands are the result of twenty years of creating a business to support his family. He didn't inherit wealth. He worked for it. What in the world are you doing?"

Fade moved onto the other hand and as with the first, he held a piece of the shiny typing paper pressed to the dead man's hand. "Whatever I'm doing isn't disturbing your husband in the slightest, Mrs. Williams."

"How dare you! Detective, I want this man removed immediately!"

"Do that and you'll regret it," Din promised. "*The Planet* stands behind Foster Fade one hundred percent in his never ending crusade against evil and injustice!"

Fade groaned theatrically. He put the papers away in a long manila envelope. He removed a small cardboard box and withdrew several pieces of chemically treated tissue paper that cleaned his hands. He wiped his hands with them, threw them into the satchel. He closed it up, put away his mechanical eyeglasses.

Emma Williams never took her wide blue eyes off of him as she said; "Fade? The Crime Spectacularist?"

"The very same," Din confirmed.

Emma Williams looked at the perplexed duo of Heath and Long. "I thought my husband had a heart attack. Why is Mr. Fade here? Doesn't he investigate murders and such? This certainly isn't a murder!"

"It certainly is," Fade said, walking between Emma Williams, Long and Heath on his way to the door, followed by Din. "I suggest you take the body to the morgue and do a proper autopsy. Check the base of his neck. I think you'll find that Williams was killed with a flechette from a needle gun. The thing is so tiny that the hole it made going in closed up immediately after penetrating the neck muscles and going right through the spinal cord with enough force to snap it right at the medulla oblongata and cause instant death."

"I suppose you saw the hole with those fancy specs of yours?" Long said sarcastically.

"Of course I did. That's why I wear them when examining a dead body. Helps me see puncture wounds that might not be apparent with the naked eye. But the thing that really interests me is the scarring on Williams' hands."

"I've already explained that," Emma said bluntly.

Fade said nothing to her, merely left the mansion, followed closely by Din, who continued scribbling in her notepad.

Outside, reclining on Fade's car was something of a surprise. The girl on the hood calmly smoking a cigarette had the demeanor of a cop herself. Silky, curly lemon yellow hair framed a high cheek boned face.

"Unless you're going to polish my entire car with that well-shaped rump, I suggest you get it up off of it," Fade said, tossing his satchel in the back seat.

The girl smiled slightly. "You're Foster Fade."

"And you're Elinor Williams, daughter of the deceased."

Elinor's smoky grey eyes opened wider. "How did you know that?"

"Not hard to figure out." Fade leaned easily on the passenger side door, the other hand fisted on his hip as he continued talking. "Saw a picture of you in your father's library. No picture of your mother but several of you. Along with all the liquor being in there I'd say he spent considerable amount of time in that library but he didn't do any reading. You came in there a lot because he's got your pictures in there."

Elinor looked at Din. "Is he serious or is he making this up to make himself sound smart?"

"When you figure it out, let me know. I'm Dinamenta Stevens, by the way. I work with Mr. Fade. I write for *The Planet*. Care to make a statement?"

"I'm more interested in what's going on in there. The detective told me to leave. Do you think there was foul play in my father's death?"

"You tell us," Fade said. "You found him. What did you see?"

Elinor shrugged, deeply inhaled smoke from her cigarette and allowed it to dribble out of her nostrils as she replied. "I didn't see anything. I came home from visiting friends upstate for a few days. I came inside, heard nothing but that didn't surprise me as today most of the staff is off. I figured Daddy was in his library. I went in, found him lying on the floor. I thought he'd fainted at first. I shook him, called his name but he wouldn't move. I then called the police."

"What time did you get home this morning?"

"Eight, eight-thirty maybe."

"Where was your mother?"

"She's always up and about early. I don't know where she was. She came home after I did. A little after nine, I think. Say nine-fifteen." Elinor looked at Fade. "Was my father murdered?"

"Why? Did he have enemies?"

"Mr. Fade, my father was worth seventeen million dollars. You don't make that kind of money without making people mad. Of course he had enemies. So was he killed?"

"Ask Coroner Long. I wouldn't want to prejudice his findings." Fade motioned for Din to get in the car. Elinor pushed herself off the hood and dropped her cigarette, mashing it under one hand made Italian pump as she watched the Packard roar away.

"What was that all about?" Din asked.

"What? I was just asking questions is all. Isn't that what I'm supposed to do?"

"You were a little more abrasive than usual."

"Let me ask you a question, Din. You're a bright girl, right?"

"That is the rumor."

"You walk into a room. You see me lying on the floor. Who do you call first? Besides The *Planet* lawyers, I mean."

"A hospital and tell them to send an ambulance, I guess."

"Why?"

"Maybe you had a seizure or something, how do I know? I'm not a doc—"

Din cut her own self off in midsentence and looked at Fade with sudden realization of what he was getting at.

"Most people, upon seeing a family member lying unconscious on the floor would call a doctor or ambulance. And in the case of the Williams family I'm just about certain that they have a family physician who's on call twenty-four hours a day. But our Miss Williams didn't think to call a doctor. Her first call was to the police. Why?"

Din's scribbling became even more furious. "Why indeed. Soon as we get back to the office I'll check on the Williams family doctor, find out who he is. Find out what kind of shape the old boy was in. But why were you so curt with Heath and Long?"

"I was curt with them because I hate sloppiness. Long's an idiot. The scarring on Williams' hands is not consistent with the scarring on his fingertips."

"I don't follow you."

"Wait until we get back to my lab and I'll show you."

FOSTER FADE'S LABORATORY always impressed Din although she'd have cut out her own tongue than admit it to him. The long tables were covered with various devices and machines that appeared to be arcane technological artifacts to her untrained eye. Fade had different sections of his laboratory devoted to different scientific disciplines. Over here where she now stood was the chemistry section where Fade practiced organic chemistry, chemical thermodynamics and theoretical chemistry. Next to the chemistry section was the physics and engineering section. Next to that resided the electro-mechanical section. And that wasn't even half of it. The laboratory took up fully half of the fortieth floor and it made Din's brain swim as she could never understand how Fade kept all the different parts of his lab straight.

Now he walked straight to a device that resembled a photographer's light table but larger in size. Fade turned it on and with a whine, the surface of the table glowed from within with a soft crystal white light. At the same time, a large screen unfolded from inside the table to lock in position.

Din watched in silence as Fade took out the two pieces of shiny typing paper and held them up for her to look at. Her lower jaw sagged in surprise. "Well cut me down and call me Stumpy!" she gulped. The papers she looked at now showed two very clear, very well defined handprints.

Fade grinned as he put the two papers on the light table. The pictures were amplified, further refined and defined and appeared on the screen in such remarkably sharp detail that every line could be seen clearly. And now Din could see what Fade meant.

"His fingertips…they don't look the same as those other scars."

"That's because acid was used on his fingertips. The palms were scarred with some sort of blade. But the purpose was served. Anybody examining Williams' hands wouldn't look very closely once they saw that his hands were so obviously scarred. They would just chalk it up that the hands were the result of years of hard work, just as the missus said."

Din cocked her platinum-bobbed head to the side. "The only reason I can think of why somebody would deliberately scar their hands with acid is to disfigure their fingertips."

"It's so rewarding to know that your association with me is not wasted," Fade said. He finger-combed his colorless hair, his eyes bright with excitement. "Add to that Williams was murdered and what do you get?"

"Our Mr. Williams had a past. Probably not a very nice one."

"Damn, Din…you're getting downright scary. You put that together without me having to lead you by the hand."

"So what do we do now, genius?"

"Get a line on the Williams family doctor. Talk to him and find out exactly what kind of health Williams was in. And after that you're going to go back and talk to little Miss Williams. Maybe some girl talk is needed right now."

Din nodded. "How about you? What are you going to be doing?"

"I'm going down to the morgue and get some background info on Williams. Despite what his daughter said about him having so many enemies, you don't kill a man just because he makes the best cider on the East Coast."

FOSTER FADE NODDED at Jenkins Gribb, the overfed keeper of The *Planet's* morgue. As usual, Gribb was eating. It occurred to Fade that there were few times he came to the morgue that Gribb wasn't eating. "How's it going, Jenks?"

"Not well for me, that's for sure." Gribb put down his tuna fish sandwich and wiped his hands on a large napkin before shaking Fade's hand. "Whatcha need?"

"Just going to poke around and get some background stuff on Philip Williams."

"The cider guy? What happened to him?"

"Dead. Din's got the story so don't mention it around, okay?"

"Sure, sure. He got himself murdered?"

"Appears that way."

"You'll catch whoever did it," Gribb said with total confidence as he returned to his sandwich. Fade walked deeper into the huge room. One of the advantages of working for *The Planet* was that Fade had access to resources that he did not have to pay for or hire other people to do for him. Such as the newspaper's morgue. In essence, he had an immense storehouse of information far more comprehensive and detailed than any filing system he could have put together. And he liked that he didn't have to keep huge file cabinets in his office. Kept it looking neater.

Fade quickly found the drawer he was looking for. Having spent many hours here, Fade did not need a lot of time to hunt up his information. He opened the drawer, withdrew the inch-thick folder full of newspaper clippings and typewritten sheets of paper and headed for the nearest table to examine the information.

Somebody already sat at that nearest table. A man of average build with deep-set brown eyes and curly gold hair. He smoked a cigarette and uncrossed his legs as Fade came closer to the table. "How you doin', Fade? Good to see you again."

"Been quite a few years, Reynolds. If we were friends I might actually be inclined to invite you around the corner to Dennehy's for a couple of drinks."

Reynolds chuckled. "Still haven't learned how to play well with others, eh, Fade?"

"I never found any others who could keep up with me is why." Fade sat down at the table across from Reynolds. "You still working for the same people?"

"Of course. Same people who keep making you an offer to come and work for them."

"I don't play well with others. What brings you here, Reynolds?"

"You working the Williams murder case?"

Fade smiled slightly. "I knew you guys were good but this is bordering on actual competence. I suppose you're going to warn me to stay away from the case."

"Quite the contrary. We're delighted you're working this case. We know you, know your capabilities. All we ask is that no matter what the resolution of the case is, you inform us first of your findings."

Fade thought that over for about 7/100ths of a second. "Williams was one of you."

Reynolds nodded. "Years ago. We set him up in the Williams identity when we retired him. The whole cider king business, though…that wasn't us." Reynolds chuckled again. "We told the damn fool to keep a low profile and he goes and becomes a millionaire. Go figure."

"So Williams worked for you—"

"Used to. Emphasis on *used to.* Williams was all the way out. He hasn't been active for twenty five years."

"So why would somebody want one of your operatives who hasn't been active in all that time dead?"

"Revenge?"

Fade shook his head. "Why wait so long? If somebody wanted revenge it certainly wouldn't have taken this long for them to catch up to him. And if it did take them that long, they certainly wouldn't be good enough to take him out, no matter how long Williams had been out of the game." Fade frowned. "It just doesn't add up. Unless you lot killed him."

"You said it yourself: why would we want one of our operatives dead after all that time? Especially when we knew who he was and more importantly, where he was. We could have killed him anytime during those twenty five years."

"I was afraid you'd say that," Fade grumbled. "This just doesn't add up."

"Which makes it right up your alley. Now you know why we're happy you're on the case. You going to play ball with us on this?"

"You need to tell me what Williams was doing for you when he was active."

Reynolds reached into the inside breast pocket of his suit jacket and withdrew several pieces of paper and passed them across to Fade. "I trust you'll properly dispose of these."

"Sure thing." Fade stood up.

"I'll hear from you?"

"When I have something to tell you. And Reynolds-"

"Yeah?"

"Just because I've agreed to help you out on this doesn't mean I'm working for your people. Let's be clear on that, okay?"

Reynolds nodded. "We're clear on that, Fade." He stood up, gave Fade a two finger salute. "Stay in touch."

"Sure." Fade watched Reynolds walk away, between rows of file cabinets, make a left and he was gone. There was no telling how Reynolds had gotten in but Fade knew for a fact that nobody had seen him come in and nobody would see him go out. Fade chewed thoughtfully on the wad of gum in his mouth as he reflected that this case had suddenly gotten a lot more interesting.

DIN BROUGHT HER Jaguar SS100 to a screeching stop. She'd passed the address she was looking for, so fast had she been going. Which was what usually happened when Din drove. Her mind was habitually on something else that had nothing at all to do with driving. It was Fade's theory that some subconscious self-preservation instinct took over and enabled Din to get to wherever it was she was going without killing herself or others.

Din backed up and parked right in front of 151 Phelps Boulevard. The brownstone housed the office and living quarters of Doctor Harold White, personal physician to Philip Williams and his family. As Din climbed out of her low-slung roadster she recalled interviewing Dr. White three or four years ago. There had been some irregularities in the daily operations of several of the city's largest and most prestigious hospitals. Mayor Ross himself had appointed Dr. White in charge of a special committee to clean things up. Dr. White had done so with a vengeance, sending quite a few hospital administrators to jail. Dr. White had impressed Din with his no-nonsense manner and thirst for justice. And it certainly was no easy job to impress Din.

She walked up to the wrought iron gate, opened it and navigated the short path to the front door. Din rang the bell and thirty seconds later the door opened. The woman standing on the other side was perhaps three or four inches shorter than Din. Twenty years older but still with a trim figure and the elegant sweep of her hair and the meticulous way she applied her makeup told Din more about the woman than she could have told herself. The woman said in a pleasant enough voice, "Good morning. Can I help you?"

"I'm here to see Dr. White. I'm Dinamenta Stevens from *The Planet*. Here are my credentials." Din opened her wallet to display her photo I.D. "I'd like to talk to Dr. White about Philip Williams."

The woman frowned. "What is going on that nobody is saying? The police called about twenty minutes ago. A Detective Heath said he wanted to question Dr. White but wouldn't say why. I demand—"

Din stepped inside forcefully, taking the woman by the arm and moving her aside gently but firmly as she kicked the door shut.

"How dare you! What is going on—"

"What's your name, honey?"

"I'm Allison Frames. I'm Dr. White's secretary and nurse."

And I'd bet next month's rent you're more than that, Din thought. *You don't put on twenty five dollars a bottle Lerone perfume just to go to work.*

"The police didn't tell you why they're coming over?"

"No! And in fact the detective I spoke to was most rude."

"Look, I'll tell you what it's about but you have to act surprised when the cops get here. Philip Williams was murdered earlier today."

"You can't be serious!"

"Saw his body myself, sister. Only person deader than Mr. Williams is Julius Caesar himself. The police are coming here for the same reason I'm here. To ask about the quality of Mr. Williams' health."

Miss Frames shuddered. "So hard to believe. Mr. Williams was just in here two months ago."

"Anything wrong?"

"No. He comes in every six months or so for a routine check-up. This was one of his regular visits. Dr. White examined him, then they sat around for about an hour having drinks and a cigar, then he left."

"Was that usual?"

"Oh, yes. Dr. White and Mr. Williams have been friends for years. I think the check-ups were just an excuse to get together to socialize. They're both such extraordinarily busy men."

"Can I talk to Dr. White for a few minutes? Before the police get here?"

Miss Frames eyed Din with open suspicion. "Why are you so anxious that you talk to Dr. White without the police?"

"You've heard of Foster Fade, The Crime Spectacularist?"

"Who hasn't?"

"I work with him. Mr. Fade is investigating his own angle on the Williams murder, independently of the police investigation."

Miss Frames nodded, her suspicion gone. "I'll be happy to assist Mr. Fade in any way I can. Please come this way."

Miss Frames led Din down a wonderfully oak paneled hallway. They passed two doors and Miss Frame explained that they led to the reception office and the examination room. The door at the end of the hall opened into Dr. White's private office. Miss Frames opened the door.

The two women gasped in shocked amazement. Dr. White lay on the floor beside his desk. If it hadn't been for one fact, they might have assumed he'd fainted and slumped out of his chair onto the floor.

But that one fact was the slim, masked figure crawling out of the window behind Dr. White's desk. The figure wore all black and the mask covering the entire head made it impossible to tell if it were man or woman. Only the malicious, baleful eyes glaring at the two women could be seen.

Din swiftly reached into her small handbag and withdrew a .22 automatic pistol. "Hold it right there, buddy!"

Buddy most definitely did not hold it right there. Buddy's arm lifted.

Din saw something black and bulbous in that hand and it was just pure instinct that made her lurch to the side, knocking Miss Frames out of the line of fire even as she squeezed the trigger of her automatic.

She heard something like angry mosquitoes zipping past her cheek as her two shots smashed into window, knocking the glass out of the frame. And then Buddy was gone.

Din reached down a hand to help Miss Frames up to her feet. "Who was that?" Miss Frames cried.

"Damned if I know. See to your boss while I check on something." Din put her gun away and turned to the wall behind her. She could see sunlight glinting off of two objects embedded in the wall. They looked like extra-long needles. Din looked around, saw a box of napkins on the desk. She took a number of them, using them to pluck the needles from the wall so that she would not get her fingerprints on them. She then wrapped the needles in more napkins to further protect them from any possible contamination.

"He's dead," Allis Frames said dully. She was kneeling next to Dr. White's body. "There's no pulse, he's not breathing."

Din walked over and placed a comforting hand on her shoulder. Din noticed that a drawer of Dr. White's file cabinet had been opened. She thought it a safe assumption that Buddy had come for Williams' health records. Well, that confirmed that Williams had been murdered as far as she was concerned. But by whom? And why?

"Look, Allison. Call the police, get them here as quick as you can. I don't think you're in any danger but you're welcome to borrow my gun if it will make you feel safer until they get here. And can I ask you for a big favor? I'd really appreciate it if you didn't mention to the police that I was here."

Allison Frames looked up at Din, tears flowing freely down her face. She managed a small smile. "If you hadn't rang the doorbell when you did, I'd probably have been in here with Dr. White and gotten killed as well. And you pushed me out of the way when that killer fired that weapon at us. So I owe you my life twice over. Of course I'll do what you asked. The police will never know you were here."

Din squeezed her shoulder. "Thanks, sister. You ever need a favor, you come to *The Planet* and ask for me." Din quickly left the office, half-ran through the hallway and out the front door. She was eager to get back to Fade's lab and tell him what happened and even more eager to put the needles in his hands.

"SO WHAT HAPPENED next?" Foster Fade asked as he held up the needles. He wore rubber gloves that protected his hand from any possible poisons on the needles as well as not befouling any substances on them. Including fingerprints. Din didn't say anything in response. Fade looked over to where she sat, knocking back a good slug of Black Pony Scotch from the fifth Fade kept in his desk. She poured herself another three fingers. "You wanna take it easy with that. It's a little early in the day to get tight. Even for you."

"It's after five somewhere in the world. And the day that a couple shots of Scotch puts me down is the day I retire and take the vows." But Din closed up the bottle and swirled the golden brown liquid around in the glass as she continued. "I've come close to getting killed a whole buncha times since I hooked up with you, Fade. That don't mean I'm getting used to it."

"Then maybe you need to find a new line of work." Fade walked over to his chemical table and placed the needles on their own separate slides and slipped them under a microscope of his own invention. He examined the needles intently. "Hm. Judging by the hole I saw in the back of Williams' neck this morning I'm positive that these needles are just like the one used to kill him." Fade looked up from the microscope at Din. "You are extremely lucky."

"Tell me about it. What else can you tell from those needles?"

Fade turned back to his microscope. "No fingerprints but it appears that some kind of residue is on the needles." He stood up, selected two test tubes. He took both needles, put them into their own tubes. He placed them inside a test tube rack and picked up a Pasteur pipette which he then used to transfer liquids from several beakers and jars into the test tubes. The liquids bubbled. "We'll let that work for a bit while I tell you about my day." Fade then related what had happened during his trip to the morgue.

Din swallowed the rest of her drink. "So who is this Reynolds?"

"All you have to know is that sometimes I work with the people he still works for."

"And just who did you work for before you signed up for this deal? I've known you for quite a while now and I know more about what's going on in China than I do about your life before you came to work for

The Planet."

"That's because there's no reason for you to know. What you do have to know is that Williams used to work for those same people." Fade passed over the papers Reynolds had given him. "And this is what he used to do."

Din read the papers quickly. She looked up at Fade, eyes wide with surprise. "Is this for real?"

"It is." Fade turned back to the test tubes. He carefully used a Pasteur pipette to remove some of the liquid in one of the tubes that had turned a milky orange. He placed a drop on a slide and placed it on his microscope. He bent down to look. For perhaps about a minute he said nothing. He stood so still that every muscle might just as well have locked into place. Finally, he looked up. "Interesting."

"You want to tell me what's so interesting?"

"There's traces of nitron on these needles. Nitron in gaseous form is used sometimes as a propellant. You say that the gun the killer used hissed when he fired? It didn't go boom?"

"Only thing that went boom was my gun as I shot back. His hissed."

"That means his gun was custom made. It doesn't fire conventional bullets so it doesn't use gunpowder. I'm betting it uses nitron capsules to fire the needles."

"Dammit, Fade, what's going on here? There's nobody who has a reason to kill Williams."

"But killed he was." Fade held out his hand for Din to give back the papers Reynolds had given him. He struck a match to them and they went up in a puff of white smoke without even leaving ashes. Fade brushed his hands together. "Fancy taking a ride back out to the Williams place?"

"Sure. We going to talk to the wife and daughter?"

"Yep. Just give me a few minutes to whip up something here, make a phone call and we'll be on our way."

"THIS HAS BEEN an extraordinarily trying day for us all, Mr. Fade. I certainly hope you have not come to add to our grief." Emma Williams certainly didn't look like a grieving widow. In fact, she looked far better than she did that morning. She sat in the library, sipping green tea. Din sat across from her while Fade stayed on his feet. He jammed his bony hands into his pants pockets and rocked back and forth, chewing his gum loudly.

"It's not my intention to do so, Mrs. Williams. But I think you can appreciate the unusual circumstances of your husband's death. That's why the police aren't here. And you know why."

Emma Williams sipped more green tea. The late afternoon sun filled the library with brilliant golden light. "I take it that you're referring to my late husband's previous job."

"I'm surprised you admit to it so easily."

"And why shouldn't I? I'm not about to insult a man with your reputation, Mr. Fade. And I'm pretty sure that you would not have brought it up unless you already knew about it. So why should we even go through the game of me pretending not to know what you're talking about?"

"How much do you know?"

Emma Williams reached for a small inlaid box, opened it and removed a cigarette. She lit it, smoked for a bit in silence before answering; "I suspected George…that was his real name, you know…George Martins. I suspected George was doing something else for a long time. He told me he was in sales and his job required that he do quite a bit of travelling. He even took me on a couple of his 'business trips' He would go out in the morning, saying he was going to meet clients and then we would meet up later for dinner and drinks, maybe take in a movie or go dancing."

"So you had no idea your husband worked as a professional assassin for the government?"

She shook her head. "None at all. Oh, I thought maybe there were other women. But George was always good to me. Never raised his hand to me. It wasn't until he quit that he told me the whole truth. He had to because we had to change our names."

"You didn't have a problem with that?" Din asked, incredulous. "Your husband killed dozens of people and you just shrugged your shoulders and went along with it?"

"Young lady, the people my husband assassinated were enemies of our country. My husband was a silent soldier who served with no uniform and no official recognition for what he did. I am proud of him."

Din started to say something else but Fade cut her off. "Argue politics and morality on your own time. I'm here on important business." Fade chewed louder, rocked back again on his heels, making them squeak. The noises were annoying but Din was used to Fade being annoying. Emma Williams frowned at him, her wish that he would stop what he was doing apparent on her face. "Namely, to catch a murderer."

"Then why aren't you out doing that very thing?" Elinor Williams walked into the library, looking as elegant as her mother. "The police certainly seem to be doing their job."

"The job of the police is to look like they're doing their job. There will be nobody for them to arrest because they have nobody with which they can hand a motive on." Fade grinned at the two bewildered women. "There's an old saying regarding murder: If you know why somebody got murdered then you'll know who did it."

"What gibberish is this?" Emma snapped.

"Get used to it," Din sighed. "It's all he talks. English is his second language."

"What it means is simply that when a man turns up murdered, the first thing you need to find out is who had the best or most profitable reason to kill that man. Philip Williams slash George Martins didn't have an enemy in the world, despite what Miss Williams told us." Fade turned his baleful colorless eyes on her. Like the eyes of a basilisk they were. "Simply put: you don't kill a man because he makes cider. It just doesn't make sense. It also doesn't make sense that he would still have enemies from his old days as a government assassin."

Elinor reached for a cigarette from the box her mother had taken one and lit it, never taking her eyes off Fade.

"You knew Daddums was an assassin, didn't you, Miss Williams?" Fade asked.

"Of course I knew. This family has no secrets from each other."

"Yes it does. Every family has secrets." Fade stopped his gum chewing and rocking back and forth. "Some are really piddling and not worth the time to think about. Others are more deadly. The secret you kept from your father was the one that got him killed."

"I'm afraid I'm going to have to ask you leave, Mr. Fade." Emma crushed out her cigarette and stood up abruptly. A sharp cry escaped her lips. Her fingers were stained a pale yellow at the tips. "What in the world—"

"Nitron propellant leaves a residue on everything. Doesn't really last long but just long enough." Fade pulled his right hand out of his pocket. He held a small silver tube with a nozzle at the tip. "Use the right chemicals, spray them in the air and it'll make the nitron residue visible."

Din jumped to her feet. "Holy jumping Jehosephat! What a story! She killed her own husband!" Then a thought occurred to Din. "Waitamminit. Then who killed Dr. White? I saw the killer with my own eyes and he was a lot slimmer and shorter than Mrs. Williams."

"That's because it wasn't my mother," Elinor Williams said quietly. Fade and Din turned to where she stood by the door, a bulbous black pistol on her hand. "All I have to do is squeeze."

"I don't get this!" Din exclaimed. "Why would you kill Dr. White?"

"I didn't want to," Elinor said. "But it was vital we get Daddy's medical records before the police got hold of them and it proved that Daddy was in perfect health. Time was of the essence."

"Still didn't have to kill him," Din muttered.

"Oh, yes she did. Elinor's never been taught anything else but how to kill people. Isn't that right, Mrs. Williams?" Fade said this to Mrs. Williams but he looked directly at Elinor.

"She's going to demonstrate that in one minute when she kills the both of you." Emma Williams smiled and this time her smile was not friendly. "Isn't it ironic? The two of you have created so many headlines but your biggest headline is going to be your sudden and utter disappearance." Mrs. Williams chuckled.

"But why kill him? What did he do to you?" Din demanded. She flung wide her arms to take in the mansion around them. "You live like royalty! You're rich! What possible reason could you have to kill him?"

"He wasn't loyal!" Emma roared. "His country needed him to come back and do the work for which he was trained to do and he refused! He laughed and said that now that he was rich he didn't have to be a government lackey!"

"And that's why you killed him," Fade said. "Your daughter killed Dr. White."

"I still don't get it!" Din exclaimed.

"You haven't figured it out yet, Din?" Fade pointed a long finger at Emma. "Sure, Williams didn't want to go back to killing for a living. But his wife and his daughter didn't mind. What did you do, Emma? Go and make a deal so that the government could have their hired killer back?"

"It wasn't supposed to happen that way!" Emma pointed at her daughter. "She wasn't supposed to call the police!"

"You didn't figure on her turning on you, did you?" Fade laughed. "Elinor did turn out to be a loyal daughter after all."

"You didn't have to kill Daddy, Momma," Elinor said. "I could have kept him quiet." She smiled at Fade. "I knew it would only be a matter of time before you caught up to her, Mr. Fade. Take her. She's my gift to you and the police. Make your case stick and use her to do so."

"We're taking both of you, young lady." Reynolds stepped into the library, a .45 automatic in one hand. He touched the brim of his hat to Fade. "Thanks for the call, Fade."

"We had a deal. You heard enough?"

"Sure did. I followed your instructions to the letter. Used the skeleton keys you left with the newsstand guy to get inside the mansion. Me and about half a dozen agents who are standing right outside waiting for me to whistle." Reynolds looked at the astounded mother and daughter. "It's all over ladies. You come with me and you'll be treated fairly."

"No!" Elinor whirled around, the deadly bulbous needle gun training on Reynolds. His weapon blasted twice. Elinor shrieked, dropped the needle gun and collapsed to the polished floor, blood bubbling from her lips. Emma screamed and rushed to her daughter's side.

Din could only shake her head. "I'll be damned. This will make a helluva story if I can figure out how to write it up."

Reynolds took off his hat as he addressed Din directly. "If it'll help, ma'am…I'd advise that you put both the murders on the daughter."

"That's just not good enough, Mr…Reynolds, right? Mrs. Williams killed her husband and she's got to stand trial for that. The girl's already paid for Dr. White's murder."

"So what's the harm in her taking the rap for a second one?" Reynolds looked at Fade. "Talk to your partner, Fade. Make her see reason."

"Not in a million years. Din and I have a deal: I solve the crimes and she writes the stories." Fade grinned.

"Miss Stevens, I'm sure you can understand why it wouldn't be in the best interests of John Q. Punchclock to learn that the United States government has employed their own cadre of trained assassins."

"Sounds like exactly the type of thing Mr. and Mrs. America need to know. And as a respected and honored member of the press-"

"Okay, okay." Reynolds held up a hand. "Tell you what…you keep any and all mention of the U.S. government involvement in this out and you can have Mrs. Williams to turn over to your local cops. We'll clean up here, take the needle gun and anything else that can incriminate the government."

Din opened her mouth to tell Reynolds where to go and what he could do after he got there when Fade's voice whispered in her ear. "Don't push it. He's giving you way more of break than he has to. As it is, he'll catch hell from his bosses."

"We got a deal, then?" Reynolds asked, holding out his right hand.

Din shook it. "We got a deal."

THE NEXT DAY, Din burst into Fade's office with the spanking brand new, hot-off-the-presses morning edition of *The Planet*, waving it over her head as if it was a flag of victory. "Didja see that headline? CRIME SPECTACULARIST SOLVES THE CIDER KING MURDER by Dinamenta Stevens! Hackrox says it's already selling like hotcakes!"

From where he sat behind his desk with his copy of the newspaper, a mug of hot coffee at his elbow, Fade wondered aloud; "Just how well and how fast do hotcakes sell, anyway? Has anybody ever done a definitive study on the speed of-"

"Oh, shut up, you! We're back in Hackrox's good graces and that's all I care about!" Din sat on the edge of his desk and rattled the headline at him.

"Shame about Mrs. Williams, though," Fade said, picking up his mug and drinking the piping hot beverage as if it were ice water.

"She never said a word, huh?"

Fade shook his head. "Nope. Not even when the cops signed her into the county booby hatch for psychiatric observation. My opinion is she's either really in a state of severe shock or a really good actress. Either way, she's going to be behind bars for good."

"Then what say we take the day off?" Din said gaily, hopping off the desk. "There's that new Tyrone Power movie I've been simply dying to see down at the Throne theater. We could-"

Din stopped as they heard the office door open. A short, chubby man staggered inside the office, holding what looked like a velour cylinder in his hands. In a wheezing, raspy voice he said, "You the Crime Spectacularist?"

Fade nodded. "That's me, chum. What's the rumpus?"

The chubby man staggered over to where Fade stood, leaving a trail of blood drops along the way. He placed the cylinder in Fade's hand and then collapsed to the floor.

"Fade, look!" Din cried. Sticking out of the chubby man's back where it had been planted squarely between his shoulder blades was a highly distinctive and ornamental dagger. For all its ornamentation it did what a dagger is supposed to do: it killed.

Fade nodded. “Looks like a sixteenth century Otsu dagger. Don’t touch it. The blades were usually poisoned.”

“What did he give you?”

“Let’s see, shall we?” Fade pulled at the velour. It was a simple covering for a two foot tall crystal cylinder. And inside the cylinder was a human eye. This human eye was very unique in size. In fact, it was the largest human eye Din or Fade had ever seen. Easily a foot in diameter.

Foster Fade grinned at Dinamenta Stevens. “I think we’ve got something here more exciting than a movie. Don’t you?”

THE END

AUBREY STEPHENS

VOODOO DEATH

AN ADVENTURE OF FOSTER FADE
THE CRIME SPECTACULARIST

- I -
AN INTERRUPTED TRIP

DEATH WALKED THE tiles of Grand Central Station. It took the form of a little man with wild hair and a desperate expression. The pupils of his dark brown eyes were completely dilated, his brown hair a mass of jagged spears pointing in a multitude of directions. His breath was rapid and shallow. As he stumbled through the wide concourse, waiting passengers moved to avoid him, mothers drew their children close.

"The drums! The drums!" His mumbled words carried to those around him. The searching eyes of his face darted here and there searching for something, someone. His hands were knotted into fists and held close to his chest as if he were gripping desperately to a secret and protecting it with his body.

Foster Fade and Din Stevens carried small cases in their hands. Din and Fade were a study in contrast. She was a tall very attractive blond and he was well over six foot and some would say he resembled a modern Ichabod Crane, but with handsome features. After weeks of nagging, Din had finally talked Fade into taking a working vacation. In between the fun and relaxation he would be dictating notes about his early career that would fill a five week run in her column about the Crime Spectacularist—known as Foster Fade to his family and friends-in their newspapers.

"Fade, hurry up! If you keep dawdling we're going to be late for the train," said Din, irritation in her voice.

"Look brat, I move at my own pace. If the train leaves, it leaves." spoke Fade.

"Oh no! Not this time. You're going on vacation and having a good time. You promised and are scheduled for six lectures. Besides, I've never been to Chicago or New Orleans. So move on, buster."

Fade picked up his pace. It was at that moment when the little man crashed into him. Fade dropped his case and with surprising ease caught the man in his arms. Fade's thin frame held a hidden strength. He eased the little man to the floor. One of the little man's hands flew to grip Fade's coat and pulled him close. A few words rushed from his mouth. "The Baron's drums pulling my soul out."

The little man's wild eyes locked on Fade, then rolled back into his head. His body went rigid and as fast as it had stiffened, it then fell limp. Breath escaped his body with a rattle. And then nothing.

Fade checked the little man's wrist and then held his palm beneath his nose. He looked up from the man to Din. "He's dead."

Din asked, "What happened to him?"

"Beats me", said Fade.

The now deceased little man's left hand dropped to his side and a small black object slipped from it and rolled to the edge of Din's shoes. Fade's quick hand snatched it in a second. Before he could examine the object, the nearby crowd drew close to the sad sight of the little man's body. Several of them began looking to Fade as if he were the one to answer all their questions about the strange occurrence.

Fade and Din looked toward the crowd. A large man wearing the uniform of the New York Police parted the whispering people. He pushed through the mob like a harbor tug shoving stubborn barges out of the way.

"All right, all right stand aside. What's the problem here? Don't you people have a train to ca...," his voice stumbled to a halt. His eyes locked on the body before him. Then just as quickly, they darted around the crowd finally returning to the body after seeing no hostile intent nearby. His glaze went from the body back to Fade and Din, seeing that they were the people nearest to the body.

"You two have any idea what's happened here? He pass out, fall, or just decide to lay down for a nap?" he inquired of them, his eyes centering on Fade.

"I'm afraid that the gentleman is deceased," said Fade. "He seemed to be having trouble walking just before he bumped into me."

"You know him?" asked the officer.

"No, never saw him before," replied Fade.

The officer looked to Din. "How about you, sister?"

"Me?" said Din, "Never saw him before in my life and wish I didn't see him now. Dropping dead like that, he took a year of my life."

The cop took notes of what they were saying only to be interrupted by a second officer arriving on the scene. "Hi Bob. Looks like a guy just decided to have a heart attack or something. You go phone for a wagon and I'll finish getting the statements and names from these folks." The second officer crossed the station to a nearby call box, while the first returned to his notes.

"Ok, you folks can go about your business, but make sure you're available the next couple of days in case any more questions come up."

"But we were going..," began Din, only to be interrupted by Fade.

"Din, the sound you hear in the distance is the 20th Century Limited heading to Chicago without us," Fade said.

"Oh Da…," said Din as Fade broke in again.

"Uh uh, be a lady, Din," he said as he handed his card to the officer. "You can reach either of us at my office number. Come on Din, back we go. You grab the bags and I'll get a cab."

Fade walked steadily to the exit leaving a fuming blonde standing by the bags. After a few moments of letting steam escape from the collar of her business dress, she bent and grabbed the bags only to look up and see the cop grinning at her.

"You can wipe that smirk off your face, flatfoot" were the icy words she directed toward him. She then walked with all the dignity of an insulted cat to the exit. As she exited the building, Din discovered that Fade had sent the cabbie to help with the bags. She saw his lanky form waiting with the cab door open. She allowed the cabbie to take the bags and then entered the open door of the cab. Fade got in beside her and pulled the door closed.

"All right wise guy, what was the big idea with the bags?" said Din, brushing a strand of blonde hair back into place.

"I wanted to get us away from there. I think there was something fishy about the little man's death, but didn't think that a beat cop would listen to me. So unruffle your feathers and I might let you hang around when I talk to Captain O'Rourke," Fade finished with a slight smile.

"Ok, you're forgiven if you spill what gives you a sense that it's not kosher."

Fade reached into his coat pocket and withdrew the small object that had rolled out of the little man's hand. "Take a look at this and tell me what you think it is." He dropped the object into Din's open palm.

Din looked down and resting there she saw what at first appeared to be a small black wad of hair. She looked closer and realized that it was thread tied around the wad so that it resembled a tiny human-like figure. There might even have been a couple of spots of some kind of paint on it to be the eyes. "Why it's like someone tried to make a little doll," she said.

"Yes, but I'm afraid it's a good bit more than that." And with that Fade clammed up, placed the figure back in his suit pocket, and sat in silence for the rest of the trip to his office.

The cab pulled to the curb in front of the Planet office building where Fade had his office and apartment on the top floor, just above the newspaper offices and next to the owner's penthouse. Fade paid the fare and then waved a five spot in front of the cabbie to get him to carry the bags into the building, up the elevator and down the hall to his office. Fade pulled an odd looking key out of his pocket, then placed it against what appeared to be a piece of smooth bronze mounted on the wall by the door. As he did, there was an audible click and the door swung partly open. Fade nudged it with the toe of his shoe to open it the rest of the way. The cabbie placed the bags inside the doorway and his eyes searched the room for who had opened the door for them seeing no one, he just shook his head, nodded to Din and Fade, then headed back to his cab.

"I think you tipped him too much just so you could show off your door," said Din.

"Now Din, you know I did it to save your poor, weak female arms from being strained. But could be you're right. Half the fun anyway." A small laugh escaped him, "Besides I needed something to lighten the day. Come on, let's go sit down and give O'Rourke a call."

They proceeded through the reception area into Fade's inner sanctum of an office. Fade slid around a large rosewood desk and into the soft black leather chair behind it. Din nimbly eased on to a corner of the desk, took a compact out of her purse and started to work on correcting her make up.

Fade dialed a number on his desk phone. In almost the time it took the rotor to finish clicking back to the start position, he heard the ringing on the other end. To his amazement in only six rings there was an answer.

"Captain O'Rourke speaking," said the voice in a fine Irish brogue.

"How are things at Manhattan North today, Liam?" asked Fade.

"I'm fine, the city is fine, and Manhattan North is fine. And Foster Fade is fine as well, I'm sure, but whatever he's after, he isn't getting," said O'Rourke, his brogue getting thicker with each word. Fade had tilted the receiver so that Din could hear. She giggled lightly at O'Rourke's rebuff. "Oh, that's fine; you've got that dizzy blonde snoop there too."

"Hey!" Din snapped.

Not put off by either one, Fade started speaking. "Now Liam, I thought you might be interested in a tidbit of information about a little man that dropped dead this morning at Grand Central Station. But if it bothers you too much to talk to me, I'll just let Din write it up in the paper and you can read it in the evening edition." There was a choking noise on the other end of the phone.

"Fade, I'll be there in less than an hour and this had better be good," replied the Captain.

Foster Fade quickly placed the receiver back in its cradle to hang up gently before O'Rourke could slam his end down in his ear. He then walked to his bookcase and started running his eyes over the titles on the lower shelf. Din watched as he pulled a book out, crossed back to his desk and began to read. At that point she knew she had lost him until he found the nugget of information he wanted. There would be no getting anything out of him for a good while. She reached into her purse and fished out a magazine that she had purchased for the train trip. She went to the plush chair by the window and began reading it to pass the time.

-2-
AN INTERESTING VISITOR

JUST OVER AN hour had passed when there was a flashing of a light on the far wall indicating a visitor at the door. Fade pressed a section of his rosewood desk and a small oval screen slid up showing a grainy picture of who was standing by the door. Fade's electric periscope revealed Captain O'Rourke standing there with a frown on his face, beside him was a dapper gentleman whose Savoy Row suit made the off-rack one that O'Rourke wore look even more drab than normal.

Din spoke out, "I'll play secretary." With that comment, she crossed into the outer office and opened the entrance door and allowed the two men to enter. O'Rourke wasted no time with a greeting, but walked through the room straight to Fade's desk. His companion followed at a more sedate pace. Din closed the door and followed as well.

"Ah, Captain O'Rourke, always a pleasure to see you," Fade said.

"Wish I could say the same," replied the Captain. "This is Mr. John Brooks. He walked into the station just after your call. He knows—er, knew the dead man and thinks that there is more to it than a heart attack."

"Oh, was it a simple heart attack?" asked Fade.

"The guy was all alone, not a mark on his body, and he dropped dead right in front of you, so heart attack, stroke, or natural causes. Plus I talked to the coroner and he agrees."

Fade made a noncommittal noise and as he did, the dapper man in the suit spoke.

"Mr. Fade, I'm John Brooks of the law firm Brooks, Brooks, and Mason. The deceased was an associate of mine. His name was Wilmer Guttman and I think he was murdered." Brooks dropped those words like a small bomb and they turned all heads to him. "Wilbur and I just returned three weeks ago from a business trip to Cuba and Haiti. Two day ago, he came into my office in a state of distress. He had received a letter threatening him. As the day went by, he grew more and more panicked. Just before leaving the office yesterday, he got a phone call. I have no idea what was said to him, but he was convinced that he was going to die."

"Well, he was right on that one," O'Rourke growled.

"Mr. Fade, Here's the rest of the problem," continued Brooks. "I received this note in the morning mail today." He handed a small piece of red paper to Fade.

Fade read the note out loud to the group. "Brooks, you're going to die a horrible death. Drop the oil business! Signed Baron Samedi." Fade looked up. "Most interesting. Does it mean anything to you Mr. Brooks and do you recognize this Samedi fellow?" asked Fade.

What's with the oil business?" chimed in Din.

"I went to Haiti as a representative for North American Oil Ltd.," said Brooks, "to work on a deal with the Haitian government to explore for new oil deposits. My older brother Theodore Brooks was supposed to go, but he was off on some adventure with his friend Lt. Col. A. B. Mayfair from the Great War. So at the last minute I went with Wilbur. We did well on the negotiations, but some minor faction that hates the current regime attempted to ruin the deal. I thought the notes were an attempt by them to bust the deal ever though we had returned to the states. As for the Samedi person, the name means nothing to me." Brooks continued, "After Wilmer's death, I realized that there was something to the threat and thought to impose on my friendship with the Police Commissioner to see if there was a chance of an investigation into the matter. He directed me to Captain O'Rourke and apparently I arrived at his office shortly after you called."

"Well, Fade," started O'Rourke, "You have any ideas about this deal? My feeling is there's nothing to it. The ruling is a natural death."

Fade stood and walked to the window for a moment. He stared into the distance, clearly thinking intently. He turned slowly to the others and spoke. "It was murder."

Brooks raised an eyebrow. O'Rourke harrumphed. Din stared as Fade pulled the small doll-like object out of his pocket. All eyes locked on his hand as he raised it to eye level and said, "This was the murder weapon!"

They all looked at him with varying degrees of disbelief on their faces. O'Rourke turned red from his hairline down to the top of his shirt. Din's glance filled with a show of worry that Fade had finally pushed himself too far. Brooks blinked several times and was the first to speak.

"Mr. Fade, this is no time for pranks or whatever you think you're doing."

Fade spoke quietly. "Din, would you be kind enough to read the bottom half of the left page in the book that I left open on the desk?" As Din walked to the book, Fade crossed to the window to stare out into the bright blue sky.

"Baron Samedi, an important figure in the Vaudoux cults of the Caribbean Islands and the southern United States, often seen as a symbol of warning and death. Most often he is drawn as a skeleton figure with a wide grin and a top hat."

"Mr. Fade," stammered Brooks, "surely you can't be suggesting that poor Wilmer was killed using magic."

"No, but I do think that Mr. Guttman thought that he was being attacked by someone using Vaudoux or as it's known in American Pulp magazines and movies, voodoo. Someone that not only attacked him, but using his terror and that small fetish doll on the desk, caused his death," replied Fade. "Judging from what you have said, I think you may be the next target for whoever did this, Mr. Brooks."

Brooks looked at Fade with a new interest. His thoughts played out visibly on his face. He looked to O'Rourke. "Well Captain, what are your thoughts on this matter?"

O'Rourke quickly answered, "What a load of.... I mean it's ridiculous killing a man with magic. Fade must be desperate to get another headline."

"I didn't say magic killed the man," Fade interjected, "just that someone used it to kill him, at least he thought that it was killing him. I really think that Brooks is in danger now." Fade crossed back to his chair behind the desk and took a seat.

"Alright Mr. Fade, who says this? I'll bear that in mind, but I tend to fall in line with Captain O'Rourke's thinking. Magic in this day and age is absurd." He paused for several seconds. "Let me review the matter for the evening and if I come to the same conclusion as you, would you be willing to undertake an attempt to discover who's behind it all?"

O'Rourke looked at Brooks and spoke. "Great! Magic, a little doll, Baron what's his name, I'm headed back to my office." He turned and headed for the door.

"Thank you for your time Mr. Fade, I'll be in touch. Miss Stevens," said Brooks, turning to Din, "I would appreciate you keeping this out of the evening paper."

Din's lips parted in a gentle smile. "No problem. I'm on vacation or at least I'm supposed to be."

As a reply, Brooks did a slight bow to both of them and said, "I believe I can find my own way out." He then walked to the door, leaving Fade and Din looking after him.

"Alright Fade," Din said, grinning, "you know more than you're letting on. And you promised to spill it to me, so cough it up. If I don't get a vacation, I'd better get a good column out of it. I can see the lead line now, 'The Crime Spectacularist' Does Magic Again! Solves the Train Station Murder!"

Fade laughed slightly. "Din, you almost have it, but the magic isn't mine. Someone killed Wilmer Guttman using what he was convinced was magic. The last thing he said as he died was that he could hear the drums and that the Baron was claiming his soul."

Din shivered as a chill ran up her spine. "Brrrrr! It felt like a goose stepped on my grave just then."

"Din, I've got a few things I need to put together from my lab. Why don't you read the chapter on voodoo in the book while I do that."

For the next hour Fade rummaged in his lab. Din finished the chapter in the book and looked on the shelves for anything else that might give her a clue, but to no avail. She saw books on everything from chemistry to aeronautics, but nothing on murder by magic. She then spent twenty or so minutes flipping through the pages of her magazine without really seeing them. The last fifteen minutes she had been doodling in her notebook drawing little dolls with evil grins.

"Fade…." Din began but the ringing of the phone interrupted her.

"Well answer it, Brat," came from the other room as Din stood to snatch the phone.

"Foster Fade's office,' she said, putting the receiver to her ear. "Just a moment, Mr. Brooks. He's in the other part of the office." Din then called out, "Fade, it's Brooks for you!"

Fade entered the room and took the phone from her.

"Yes, Mr. Brooks," he said holding the receiver so that Din might hear as well.

"Fade, you have got to help me!" John Brooks spoke as if he was about to panic. "I'm calling from a phone booth near my club. It's for real. I left my office early and was walking to my club just down the block, when I was bumped into by a man and found something pushed into my hand. I looked and there was a folded note. I turned to see who had given it to me, but the man had disappeared in the early evening crowd."

Fade spoke in a calming voice. "What did the note say?"

Brooks continued in a more sedate tone. "You are marked, John Brooks. Baron Samedi will take your soul unless you change your ways. Don't help the evil ones that are stealing the lifeblood of the Haitian people. You have two days to make amends. Look to your soul. The Baron is watching you."

"It's not too different from the threat Guttman received and does give you a time limit," said Fade.

"But Fade, you don't understand. When I finished reading and looked for the man, I could have sworn that I heard drums. Then I looked all around and I saw something move in a dark alley next to me. My God, Fade, I looked and it was the figure of a man. I took a couple of steps toward him and noticed that he was wearing a top hat. At that very second, he looked up from the shadows at me and he had the face of a skull. It was like someone had struck me. I was dizzy for several seconds and when I looked back at the alley he was gone. You must help me!"

"I shall," Fade answered quickly, "but you must do exactly as I say."

"Whatever you say, Mr. Fade," Brooks replied hurriedly.

"First, call Captain O'Rourke and have him send a squad car to your location. Let the officers take you home and if you can, talk O'Rourke into having one of the officers stay with you for the night. Do your best not to worry. I have some ideas and will contact you as soon as I known more."

"Thank you, Mr. Fade. I shall do so now." Brooks hung up.

"Wow," said Din as Fade returned the receiver to its cradle.

"Things seem to have heated up quickly," agreed Fade. "I do have some ideas and a partial plan. Din, I want you to go home and get yourself ready for a night on the town. I'll be by to pick you up at eight. Dress in your high society evening wear."

Fade picked the phone up and pushed a button on it. He waited until the doorman of his building answered.

"Henry, Mr. Fade here. Miss Stevens will be coming down shortly. I would greatly appreciate you having a taxi waiting for her." Fade listened for a moment to the voice on the other end, then put the receiver back in its cradle. "Henry will have a cab for you, head on down."

Din crossed to the door. She turned back to Fade and said, "I hope you know what you're getting us into. This thing is giving me the willies."

Fade watched as she walked out the door into the hallway. He turned and walked back through the office and out to the living area of his apartment crossing into the bedroom. He went to the closet and removed his eveningwear, placing it on the bed. He stared at it and spoke to himself. "I wonder if I should wear a top hat?" His laugh over this echoed slightly as he headed to his bath.

-3-

OUT FOR THE EVENING

FADE POCKETED THE last of his gadgets in his suit pockets, glanced again at his top hat and shook his head slightly. He did reach for the stout blackthorn walking cane just inside the closet door. He twirled it once and, satisfied with his choices, he checked himself in the full-length mirror on the back of his bedroom door. He decided that he was correct for the evening and opened the door and walked through it to his office. He quickly called the doorman to flag a cab for him in five minutes. He passed into the outer office, through the door, setting his special electric alarm as he did so. He turned to the right and walked to the express elevator, entered it and shortly was in the lobby of the building. George, the night doorman, had a cab pulled up to the curb waiting for him.

He stepped into the cab and said Din's address aloud. The driver slid smoothly away from the curb. Fifteen minutes later, the cab arrived at her apartment building. Fade told the driver to wait, and then walked up the steps to the call box. He pressed the button below Din's name. A few seconds later her voice came through the speaker.

"Yes?"

"Hello beautiful, it's your urban knight in cloth armor come to whisk you away to an enchanted evening under the starry New York sky," Fade said with a sarcastic lift in his voice.

"I'll be right down," replied Din laughing.

Within three minutes the door opened and Din came out. A slinky, black silk dress clung tightly to her very pleasing form. In the circle of light at the building's door, she bore a resemblance to Jean Harlow. Though her hair was a darker blond, her face had the same fine features. The low cut neckline made it very clear that she was a well-formed woman and drew admiring glances from the few men passing by as well as the cabbie.

"Wow! I see why the riot started," said Fade. "Your chariot awaits." Fade took her arm and they both went to the taxi and entered. As they sat, Fade said to the driver, "Connie's Inn, please." The driver glanced at Fade in the rearview mirror, but put the cab into gear, shifted into first and headed to Harlem. Night descended fully as the cab crept though the streets working its way between the mass of people headed to the evening attractions. As they crossed over into Harlem, the traffic grew lighter and remained that way until they reached the block where the club was located.

The cab pulled to the curb and a doorman open the rear door to allow Fade and Din to exit. Fade turned back briefly to pay the driver. He then took Din's arm and entered the club through the open door giving the doorman a nod of thanks as they passed him.

Standing in the club proper, Fade and Din surveyed the twenty five or so tables, mostly occupied, around them. They were placed in a U shape around a dance floor and a middle size stage squatted on the far side. The jazz poured from the stage to flood their ears.

The Maître d' came to them as they were looking over the crowd. Fade introduced him to a picture of Andrew Jackson held in the palm of his hand and quickly found that they were shown to an empty table midway to the stage. Fade and Din took their seats. Din peered into the shadows attempting to discover who was enjoying the show. Looking closely at a table in the corner by the stage, she turned to Fade and said, "Fade," drawing his attention to the man at the corner table, "Is that really Dutch Schultz?"

"Yes and that's really Babe Ruth at the table just to the right of him. Look on the other side of the stage floor and you'll see John Barrymore and his wife." Their attention was soon drawn to the stage. They had entered during the first half of the floorshow and the performance was warming up. The latest performer had just begun. He had a round shaped face and wore a large grin as he put down the trumpet and began to sing in a raspy baritone voice. As he finished his song, he caught sight of Fade in the crowd and looked directly at him and gave a brief nod and a wink. Seeing that he had been recognized, Fade sat back and began observing the crowd. Soon a waiter appeared at his side and after consulting with Din, he placed an order for a light meal and drinks for them both.

Din was fascinated with the floorshow and paid little attention to the meal. After the first act drew to a close, a small band took the stage and began to play dance music. Several couples moved to the floor and began to swing to the music. Out of the shadows the trumpet player moved into one of the empty seats at their table.

"Hiya, Pops," he said to Fade. "I got your message."

"Din, I'd like to introduce you to Mr. Louis Armstrong," spoke Fade.

"Oh, no mister please, such a lovely lady must call me Satchmo," he said beaming.

"Alright," said Fade, "down to business. Din, I met him a few years ago when some of our local hoods attempted to blackmail some of his band members. Afterward when we were having a couple of drinks he told me a few stories about Marie Laveau and weird happenings when people use of her Vaudox in New Orleans. So, I called Louis in the hopes that he might know someone that could fill us in better about this vou dou stuff."

"Well I don't know about hope, but I ain't happy about telling you what I do know," Armstrong said frowning, "I used to hear all kinds of rumors in Naw 'leens. A lot of it not good things. But I don't know enough to tell you much, so I kinda asked around and got a name for you. A friend called the guy and he's willing to meet you tonight."

"Excellent!" said Fade.

"You really should think about taking the lady home before you meet him," Armstrong replied frowning.

"Satchmo, the lady can take care of herself," said Din.

Satchmo held his strong hands up in a surrender gesture. "Ok toots, it's your call. Ya'll see the drummer." Fade and Din looked to the stage. "His name is Willie and right after the second half of the show, he'll take you to the meeting." His face breaking out into a big grin, Armstrong reached across the table and shook Fade's hand as he stood to leave. "Well back to the gig, you take care, toots, and you keep an eye on her." He walked to the side curtain of the stage and disappeared from view behind it.

"You have the most interesting friends. But he seems like a very nice man," said Din.

"He is. I liked him when we first met a few years ago in Chicago."

Fade and Din settled back to watch the rest of the performance.

An hour later the drummer called Willie glided up to the table.

"Mr. Fade?" he said.

"That's me," said Fade, "and you're Mr. …?"

"Willie, just Willie," replied the drummer. "I'm your guide for a short trip."

"Off we go then,' said Fade. With that the couple got up and followed the thin, nervous young black man. He led them out the door of the club and into the streets of Harlem.

-4-
INTO THE DARK

WILLIE LED THEM past apartment buildings, clubs, and sometimes a combination of the two. After traveling several blocks he reached the one he was searching for and turned down an alley in the center of it. They continued down the alley until they stood before a narrow door with a dim light above it. Willie spoke softly. "This is the place. It's a private club called The Dungeon. I'll get you past the door, but you'll have to pass a little lettuce to the woman that answers. Ask her for a man named Duvalier and as a favor forget that I exist."

"What was your name again?" said Fade with a smile. Willie gave a slight laugh, turned, and knocked on the door. It opened a crack and he spoke a few words, nodded once. He then walked off down the alley disappearing into the dark of the night. The door opened all the way and a hand with long, thin fingers beckoned them enter. They did so. Fade turned to discover that the hand was attached to a woman's arm. He placed a twenty dollar bill in the open palm. Fade asked for Mr. Duvalier. The woman didn't speak but led them further into the room. As their eyes adjusted, they saw the décor of the "club."

The basic color was black with areas of blood red. The club's name became very easily understood. The booths with their tables were designed as small cells with shackles and chains on the walls. The woman silently brought them to a table in the shadows near a small stage. Sitting there was an elegantly dressed black man with a look of superiority.

Fade said, "Mr. Duvalier?"

"Francois Duvalier at your service," the man said as he rose to his feet. He extended a hand to Din, inviting her to take a seat. "But please call me Doc. I've been in the Midwest taking some advanced classes. I learned there that doctors are often referred to by that nick name by their friends and I do wish us to be friends." As he spoke they noticed that he had an accent with elements of both French and English, yet was neither and had an overlay of something else.

"Doc, it's a pleasure to meet you," said Fade.

Din smiled and passed on the same sentiments.

Fade inquired, "You have an interesting accent. May I ask what it is?"

Doc spoke, "I'm Haitian. I should have told your friend Louis to tell you why he was sending you to me. In Haiti I've had experience with Vou Dou. So if you tell me your worries, perhaps I can help you."

Fade quickly gave him the background information leaving out some of the names of the people involved. As he finished he looked to Doc to see his reaction and hopefully find some help. Doc sat motionless intently thinking. At last he said, "There are many in Haiti that do not care for your country being involved with mine. One of these people with power has engaged a bokor, a worker of Vou Dou who cast spells. A man who would use its power for evil, a bad man, one of those that you have heard the stories about making zonbi." He cleared his throat. "Zombies."

"This man Brooks," Duvalier continued, "that you spoke of is in great danger. The Wilmer person…there's a danger he may come back as a zombie. The bokor has called on Baron Samedi to destroy Brooks and claim his soul. And you said he saw Baron Samedi. If he has, the Baron will visit him tonight. I am afraid you may not believe me but I assure you that there are zombies. I have seen them in Haiti. I have watched the making of the zombie dust." His accent grew thicker the longer he spoke. "Mon dieu! Il doit être Le Colonel Gast."

"Easy there, Doc, English please," said Fade quickly

Doc continued, "I have just realized who may be doing these things. When I arrived at the train station earlier in the week I thought I saw somebody that I recognized from Haiti. But I convinced myself that I had to be wrong and it was just a man with a passing resemblance. There is a man called Paul Gast that mothers tell stories to scare their children with to get them to behave. Telling them that the Gast man will come and take their heads."

"Gast was a private in the Caco army during the rebellion. When the

United States Marines were sent to Haiti, he fled to the mountains and over a period of years gained some followers. After the revolt failed and the occupation was put in place, he became a bandit leader and began practicing Vou Dou. He was known for taking the heads of men that opposed him and he could make zombies. There was a young Marine named Puller that was made a lieutenant in the Gendarmerie d'Haiti, the national police, who put a price on his head. It was then that he began calling himself Colonel Gast to outrank his foe. He sent three men to Puller and the story is that they ambushed him and charged at him waving machetes. Puller stood his ground, drew his pistol and calmly shot three times, dropping a man with each shot. They were the enforcement squad for the "Colonel". It gave him a hatred for all Americans and he has sworn revenge on any that interfere with his plans for Haiti.

"You think you saw him here in New York?" asked Fade.

"I'm almost certain I did. The man will stop at nothing. If he wants your Mr. Brooks dead, he will die." The more Doc spoke, the more nervous he became. "Mr. Fade, I …I think I must leave you now. I have family I must think of and this man would not stop for a moment in killing them if he finds out I've helped you." He stood up to leave. "Be very careful if you attempt to stop him and take the young lady home. Good night." He turned and walked quickly away before Fade or Din could say another word.

Din was staring at Fade and turning very pale.

Fade said, "We need to get to a phone." They stood, Fade dropped a ten spot on the table and they headed for the front door. As they did many eyes were on them. The woman that had lead them to their table was nowhere in sight. They exited the club and began the walk back to Connie's Inn. Fade used the streetlight to pull his watch out of his vest pocket. "Just a little after eleven, I'd say that now is the perfect time to call our friend O'Rourke.'

Din let go with a small laugh that was more relief than humor, but nodded a definite yes to the idea. They soon walked the short distance back to Connie's Inn. There under the corner streetlight Fade saw a phone booth. They walked to it and he bent his thin frame into the booth and settled on the seat. Dropping a nickel into the phone slot he dialed Captain O'Rourke's home number.

"O'Rourke." said the voice on the other end of the line.

"Fade here, Captain. I've just left a meeting and the information I received makes it fairly sure that Brooks is in danger of some type of attack tonight."

"Really?" O'Rourke replied sarcastically. "Someone tried to break in to his house half an hour ago. You're just a little late with the warning. I'm headed to his home now."

"I'll meet you there," Fade replied. "Let me have his address." Getting the information requested, Fade hung up. He checked the street and luckily several cabs waited in front of the club for the crowd leaving the second show. Fade and Din crossed to one and were soon speeding to the address Fade had been given.

-5-
THE BARON STRIKES

FADE ATTEMPTED TO talk Din into being dropped off at her apartment, but it was to no avail. She was determined to be in on the story as it happened. As they pulled up to Brooks' home they saw Captain O'Rourke just getting out of his car and a foot patrol officer speaking to him. Fade and Din walked to the Captain's car.

"Alright, Mr. Crime Spectacularist, come on along, maybe you can help," said O'Rourke as they started toward the home's front door. "According to the on scene officer Brooks started acting strange at ten and shortly after the officer heard a clock chime half past the hour, Brooks yelled 'He's here!' Then he rushed to the officer and tried to grab his revolver." The small group reached the door and the officer with them opened it for them.

Inside they saw Brooks and a second officer standing in the entrance hall. "I'm telling you I saw it, a skeleton wearing a top hat and pointing at me. Oh God I'm going to die and I think I can hear the drums. Wilmer heard them and he's dead!" Brooks was almost yelling. He suddenly seemed to collapse into himself and grew quiet.

"Mr. Brooks, why don't we all go to your study?" suggested Fade. "We'll all be with you. You'll be very safe there."

Brooks led them down the hall to a large bookshelf lined room. He walked over to a plush leather chair by a large desk and folded into it. Fade and O'Rourke walked to either side of him, while Din looked around the room and went to a set of French doors to peer into the night beyond them. As Fade and O'Rourke reassured Brooks, Din saw a motion in the garden outside the windows. She leaned close to the window to try and see further into the dark. As she did she became sure that something moved there. Very silently she moved her hand to the release and pushed the doors open. She stepped out into the night.

Suddenly, she was confronted by a giant skeletal figure reaching for her. Her scream echoed into the room behind her. The bone hands tried to grasp her throat. She threw her arms up to protect herself, stumbling back as she did so. She felt hands grab her and she was pulled into the blackness.

Fade and O'Rourke rushed to the doors. They got there in time to see a flash of Din's blonde hair as she was pulled into the lurking shadows. Fade pulled a small object from his pocket and O'Rourke grabbed for his service revolver. Fade's long legs outdistanced the Captain easily. With his eyes adjusting to the moonlight, Fade saw Din struggling with someone, while being dragged down a path leading away from the house.

Fade gained on them. Suddenly and without warning a giant figure loomed before him. Fade saw a glowing skeleton that stood even taller than him, over seven foot in height. In its spectral right hand he saw the gleam of metal.

Fade ducked. As he did so a razor sharp machete cut through the space that his neck had occupied moments before. The skeleton started to laugh with an eerie, hollow sound.

"I'm Baron Samedi. I shall take your head here and then take your soul to hell."

Fade drew back and put his cane between the figure and himself.

"I'm Foster Fade and I don't think I'll let you do either."

O'Rourke caught up with Fade as he spoke. The skeleton seemed to flicker in the night. There one moment and gone the next. It reappeared closer to them and had drawn the machete back ready to cut again. The Captain started to aim his revolver. Instead of a cut the machete hurled threw the air headed for O'Rourke's arm. The Captain flinched. The blade missed his arm, but connected with the barrel of his revolver, which went spinning off into the dark.

Before Fade or the Captain could do anything else the thing had vanished and along with it so had Din and whoever had her. In the distance they heard a car pulling away. Fade had the flashlight on now and O'Rourke spotted his gun and grabbed it. Both men then rushed around the end of the building and into O'Rourke's car. He threw the car into gear and accelerated down the road in the direction the car was going. As the Captain hurled his auto around a curve, Fade thrust out a finger to point toward a set of bright red tail lights. O'Rourke pushed the powerful police sedan to its limit and was soon gaining on the fleeing apparition, the unknown assailant, and the kidnapped Din.

The cruiser pulled closer to the speeding villains. Fade saw the car's desperate turn onto a dirt road next to a bridge. Without a word Captain O'Rourke swung his vehicle on to the same turn. His car wildly fishtailed but kept its traction and was once more narrowing the distance between the two vehicles. The fleeing car crashed into a clump of bushes next to the road. The Captain aimed his car for the same space though he did slow as it hit the brush. Fade, straining to see in the rolling headlight beams, watched the other car come to a halt next to a small creek. Coming out of it was a man grasping a struggling Din. They were soon followed by another dimly see figure.

The police cruiser slid to a stop near the other car's rear bumper. Fade sprung from the car with O'Rourke closely behind him. They ran in a ground eating trot to the small creek in time to see the skeletal figure turn to them. They could also see the man holding on to Din. She made another attempt to escape his hand. He drew back his right hand and delivered a blow to her. She went limp. Fade cried out and headed straight for Din's captor. As he saw the two pursuing men heading in his direction he reached into his pocket. They heard him call to the apparition, "Kill them, now!!"

O'Rourke yelled to Fade, "You get that guy, I'll take care of Mr. Bones."

Fade made a try at throwing the villains off by yelling, "Give it up, Gast! We've got you and know everything."

"You know nothing," he yelled back. "You'll both die here!" In an attempt to make his words come true, he rushed toward Fade and O'Rourke. As he drew close his hand came out of his pocket holding a small jar. With one twist of the lid from his free hand it opened. His right hand pulled back and he let fly with it. The jar was over their heads in a moment and a fine white dust carried by the wind blew into their faces. O'Rourke veered more to his left still aiming at the skeleton. Fade pulled to a halt pulling his hand out of his pocket and putting it to his face. The dust settled on him. As Fade rushed forward he heard a smack of a fist and a grunt from O'Rourke. Out of the corner of his eye he saw the Captain slump to the ground, his arms wrapping around the bony figure as he did.

Fade resumed his run toward Gast. He was still gripping his cane tightly, prepared to use it a weapon if needed. Gast bent to pull at one of his shoes. He straightened up clutching a straight razor in his hand.

"Die Yankee pig!" screamed the enraged Gast.

Fade swung his cane in an arch that would have done a professional baseball player justice. The hard blackthorn connected with the side of Gast's head. "Actually," Fade said, "I'm more of a Dodger fan." Gast hit the ground stunned and out cold. As he did Fade felt the cane ripped from his hand. He whirled to see the skeleton looming over him. The figure's bony hand reached up to its head and gave a tug. Some type of a mask came off revealing a face grinning in anticipation. A grin that turned into a snarl as the huge figure spread its arms wide, ready to crush life from the smaller man before him. Fade was nearly as tall as his assailant but in the flickering light from the moon, he could tell that the shoulders concealed in the skeleton suit were much wider than his and the chest was the size of a barrel.

Fade backed away, reaching for his inside coat pocket. The giant before him tossed the cane far from both of them. With no weapon, the giant reached for Fade with hands that could easily span a dinner plate. Fade saw that gloves covered the giant's hands. The giant opened and closed his fingers. He got to Fade and the grasping hand gripped the lapels of Fade's suit. This put him just where Fade wanted him. From his pocket Fade had removed a six inch long Bakelite tube. He rapidly removed a rubber cap from one end to expose two small copper prongs.

The giant was strong but Fade was faster. His right hand shot up, thrusting the end of the tube with the sharp little prongs into the perspiring cheek of the giant. There was a loud crackle. The giant froze as his entire body went tense. Fade pull the tube away from his face. There were two small punctures and drops of blood. The giant hands released Fade. Then the giant›s eyes rolled up into his head. With the sound of a tree falling and landing, he smashed to the ground and stopped moving.

With a deep release of breath, Fade turned to make sure that Gast was still down. Seeing no movement from him, he moved swiftly to Din's side to check on her. She stirred as he got to her. He bent to raise her to a sitting position. Her eyes flickered open.

"What happened?" asked Din. "Where did he go? I'll show him what happens to guys that hit ladies."

"I'm afraid you'll have to wait on that," Fade said. "Can you stand?"

Din nodded a yes and he helped her up. She looked around and saw the two men lying on the ground. "Your work?" she said.

"Yep but what happened will have to wait. I need to see if O'Rourke is ok."

Fade walked to the policeman. He spoke to him several times and finally, after nearly five minutes, got an intelligent reply. His first words were, like Din's, also as to what had occurred. Fade once again started to explain that it would have to wait. Just then the second patrol car pulled up, lights flashing. An officer stepped out of the car. O'Rourke had recovered enough to direct him to go handcuff the two criminals. He stepped to the giant.

"Hey Cap', this guy doesn't need the cuffs. But, he will need a ride to the morgue."

"Alright," O'Rourke said, "call that in after you get the other one cuffed and in the car."

Fade helped Din into the car as O'Rourke walked to them. All three watched as Gast was cuffed and placed in the back of the patrol car. O'Rourke said, "Let's head back to Brooks' place and get this straight for my report." They made the trip back much slower than the one out.

-6-

SECRETS REVEALED

FADE, DIN, O'ROURKE, and Brooks were all in the study of Brooks' mansion. Fade began his recounting of the rescue of Din and the capture of Gast.

"What was the nut case throwing at you?" O'Rourke asked. "The last I remembered was that giant hitting me and trying to hold on to him and next thing you were standing there talking to me.'

Fade replied "I'm not exactly sure what the precise composition of it is but it was the zombie dust that Duvalier told us about. I'm sure that the dust that hit me was some kind of hallucinogenic drug. I've no doubt that poor Wilmer was given a large amount. The same would apply to Mr. Brooks."

"But why didn't it have any effect on you?" asked Din.

Fade reached to his nose and removed two small circular objects. "Nasal filters, a little toy of mine, but they kept the dust out of my system. Before you ask," Fade said, pulling the small device he'd used earlier from his coat, "this is what did the giant in, a portable capacitor that a friend and I designed. Remind me Din, I must tell Nikola that it works fine but may be a tad dangerous. And speaking of the giant, he wore a black suit with the skull and bones painted on it in phosphorus. When he wanted to disappear he just turned sideways or so that his back was to the viewer. The poor giant was recruited at some point by Gast to replace the enforcement squad that Captain Puller put out of business in Haiti. The use of the suit allowed Gast to have even more control over those that would believe in Baron Samedi."

Brooks looked to Fade and said, "Any idea of why they were after me?"

"My guess would be a general dislike of Americans and specifically to destroy your business there. Perhaps with interrogation Gast will reveal more." Fade looked to the Captain.

"I'll put him through the wringer later today," O'Rourke guaranteed. "But for now I think it's time for all of us to call it a night."

THE NEXT DAY, Fade sat in his office watching Din read through her latest article in the latest edition of the Planet.

"Happy with your story?" Fade said. He saw her nod. "It was nice of you to give O'Rourke a little credit." Another nod. "How about I take you out for a nice relaxing supper? Just food, no meetings, weird happening or people dropping dead." She looked at him with that comment and again nodded. "Is there some reason you're not talking?"

"My jaw is still swollen and it aches," she mumbled.

"You mean I might get through a meal with you without a couple of dozen questions?" That gained Fade a growl. Din took out her compact to check her make up. "Come on, Brat. I was thinking we can still take a vacation. You know go someplace with warm weather and sandy beaches.....Hmmmm....I hear Haiti is nice."

Fade made it out the door just before the compact sailed through the space where he had been standing.

DAVID WHITE

THE PIED PIPER OF HARLEM

AN ADVENTURE OF FOSTER FADE
THE CRIME SPECTACULARIST

MIDNIGHT FELL ON New York, this night no different from the many that came before it. The sky was clear and the full moon glared brightly down on Officer Michael McKettrick. He was making his usual rounds and checking the usual spots. He checked doors of storefronts to make sure they were locked. Shined a flashlight into others just to take a peek at some of the stuff he couldn't afford. He whistled merrily as he twirled his night stick. It was a grand evening, and though it took time from the Missus and the kids, Michael really enjoyed walking the night beat.

He was just passing the 42nd St. National Bank when he heard a clanging from a darkened gangway that separated the Bank from its neighboring building. He pulled his flashlight from its pouch on his hip and shined it down the darkened space. The buildings behind and next to it were taller, so there was no light from the street or moon. The gangway jogged slightly toward the back so he cautiously stepped in. His light bounced off the stone and stucco covered walls as he moved inward. He undid the snap on his service revolver just in case something was wrong. Probably just some bum looking for a place to crash, but one never could tell.

Mckettrick was a good cop but he had yet to be truly tested. Called Lucky Mike by the other men in his precinct, he had never gotten involved in a tough case or dangerous situation over a career spanning fifteen years. It was this fact that now had him sweating bullets, his hands clammy and moist. He could count on one hand the number of times he had needed to draw his gun. He swallowed a breath and moved further in.

He was just coming to the spot where the gangway jogged, when a loud rustling sound gave him a start. His already sweaty palms lost the grip on the flashlight. As it fell, the cones of light bounced around the walls before going out, leaving McKettrick in the dark. He bent down to find the flashlight to see if it still worked but the hairs on the back of his neck stood up. It was then Mike McKetterick realized he wasn't alone.

He raised his head and saw what looked like several dozen small red eyes. All fixed on him. RATS!

He struggled to get his gun out and jump to a standing position, but his nerves got the better of him as he stumbled backward to the ground. He finally worked his gun free but never got the chance to raise it. A loud orchestra of screeches and whines filled the gangway, the pitter-patter of hundreds of little feet descending on him.

McKettrick beat at some and kicked at others, but for every one he hit it seemed three more took its place, scratching and sinking long razor sharp teeth into his flesh. He tried to scream but slimy rodents covered his whole face. He felt his flesh and muscle being chewed from his body bit by bit. Eventually, darkness mercifully claimed him…Lucky Mike was lucky no more!

THE FORTIETH FLOOR of the *Planet* Tower was home to a unique individual. The frosted glass window that grabbed attention said in bold letters, FOSTER FADE-CRIME SPECTACULARIST. Not detective, nothing so ho hum… but SPECTACULARIST. That was what the *Planet* paid him such a healthy paycheck to be. The *Planet,* being one of the most read papers in the world—a fact that netted its owner Gubb Hackrox a cool five million annually—wanted Fade to solve crimes that were thrilling and beyond the police. There was no place for the mundane crime. The readers of the Planet demanded mystery and intrigue and that is what Fade gave them.

Fade sat at the large mahogany desk in his large modernistic office. The walls were lined with sleek panels dotted with shiny chrome strips set in different patterns. The rug was a deep nap with large lines as well as circled patterns. Fade had a pair of his large shoes sitting on the desk in front of him. He had just gotten them back from one of several mechanics the *Planet* kept on a payroll to build the futuristic devices Fade came up with. He was tinkering with a tiny screwdriver when the phone rang. He grabbed it from its hanger, answering in his usual elegant if not somewhat arrogant tone.

"Foster Fade—the man who taught Sherlock Holmes almost everything he knew, no wait, strike that, everything he knew."

"Fade, this is Nate Basker. I…er… have a hot tip for ya on something that just broke last night. If'in ya hurry, you can get here in time to look over the scene nice'n fresh, see?"

“Well what the hell are you waiting for, you rummy? Give it to me straight, man.”

“Well I was think’n that…”

“Now there’s two things that don’t go together Nate, you and thinking. Now quit wasting what is highly valuable time and give. The usual finder’s fee will apply, don’t worry that little thing that passes for a brain of yours.”

Nate gave Fade the information on the mangled cop and the address of the 42nd St. National Bank. Fade slammed the receiver down in the hanger and sprang from his seat. He stood nearly seven feet tall, but was gaunt and cadaverous. The loose fitting suit, though being finely tailored, was still in need of at least fifty pounds to help fill it in. His pale complexion extended straight through his eyebrows and across his hair. He moved to a specific panel and touched his forehead to one metal strip and the finger on his left hand to another. This completed some intricate contacts and the panel quietly slid open, revealing a secret compartment. Fade was like a kid in a candy store. Every time he used one of his secret compartments, it brought a grin to his face.

The compartment was just one of many that housed some of the gadgets that Fade’s mind had thought up and his mechanics had built. He grabbed a black duffle bag and quickly picked out a few items and placed them inside. When finished, he placed the forefinger of each hand on another two strips and as quietly as the panel had opened, it slid closed.

He took two long strides to reach the door of the reception area and with a swift arc swung it open. The reception area housed a smaller desk and a few modern art deco pieces of furniture. It also housed a certain platinum blonde with shapely curves in all the right places and a bronze tan. Her name was Din—short for Dinamenta—Stevens and she was the storyteller of the spectacular crimes that Fade solved. It was her niche in writing and she was quite good at it. Gossip and regular news never held her interest, but her skills at this job garnered a wage higher than the assistant editor. A fact she was not shy about letting people—Fade at the top—know about.

Fade flowed into the room in his straight standing snobbish manner. Din paid him no attention as she blew on what appeared to be freshly polished nails. Fade shook his head as he spoke.

“Listen Princess, if it wouldn’t be too much of a bother I need you to head over to the 42nd St. National Bank with me and take some pictures.

I just got…" he was cut short.

"Busy here, in case you didn't notice. Just got a fresh manicure, and with what the boutique charges, I need to let them dry."

Fade's pale features were suddenly a bright shade of red as he spoke. "Well by all means let's not keep the world spinning while that happens, you little trollop. But don't fret. I am sure one of the copy boys can probably do a more bang up job anyway."

Fade dashed past platinum Din's desk and out the door, slamming it hard behind him. His long strides carried him to the elevator where he banged the button home. The doors promptly opened to reveal a young red headed and freckle faced young man. "Morning Mr. Fade, how's the crime solving business going?"

"It would be going much better if a certain platinum haired hussy spent more time working and less time fluffing up her image, Arthur."

The boy called Arthur had worked there long enough to expect the tiffs that went on between Foster and Din. He also knew better than to add in his two cents. He quietly slid the doors closed and sent the elevator hurtling toward the lobby. The ride was quick, but there were no shortages of curses spewed from under Fade's breath. Arthur just nodded in agreement, wanting the ride to be over with.

Din was still in her chair, casually blowing on her nails and whistling without a care in the world. She casually grabbed up the phone from its cradle and dialed a number. When the voice on the other end picked up she spoke briefly and straight forward. "James, I need you to be a darling and bring the car around for me. It would seem Mr. Spectacular needs my assistance at the 42nd National Street Bank." She placed the phone back on its hanger and bent down to open up the bottom drawer of her desk. She reached in and removed her state-of-the-art camera. She placed it in her carrying case and got up to leave the reception area. As she passed the large mirror that she had insisted be placed on the wall, she couldn't help but stop and stare at her reflection in the mirror.

"You, my darling, are one hot number." She blew herself a kiss and hustled out the door to meet the driver.

HARLEM WAS OVER-CROWDED and rapidly becoming dilapidated. It was in the dank basement of one of the recently condemned buildings that a small bulb glowed. A man sat in his wheelchair working feverishly at a table that was made of a piece of rotted plywood set atop some empty milk crate. The man was Artemis Gray. An African American who was driven to make himself known, to be allotted the same chances in life as the white man. His near black skin was covered with a layer of sweat, his emaciated face looking as if he belonged in a morgue. The copper eyes though, glared not only with a show of intellect but also with a burning desire to get even.

It had been two years since the dreaded fever almost claimed his life and left him an invalid. But the fever, for all the harm it had inflicted on his body, had helped him tap into the vast areas of the brain that most never used. It had made his mind a tool of genius. He was no longer a dullard as he admitted he had been before, a 'dimwit' as many called him. Memories of the past, the insults merely added fuel to what was already a blazing inferno that raged within his soul. He would show them—show them that he was smarter and better than all of them. Better than every last one of the people that doubted him and kicked him when he was down.

He tinkered away on an electronic device with wires and small tubes. He spliced and he taped. He smiled to himself as he soldered the last connection. The fever had opened up his mind; things just came to him now. Ideas, plans, it was these things that he would use to raise himself up from the filth of the gutters he was once dumped in and left to die. He set the soldering iron down. A thin lipped smile formed on his face as the rotted door of the basement dwelling thudded open with a loud creak.

The man who came through was a bit out of place in any venue. He stood only four feet tall, but was nearly just as wide. He had an enormous head and his arms nearly scraped the floor. His hands were at least twice the size of a normal man's, every spot of his dark skin showing corded muscles that were even more powerful than they looked.

His name was Rosco and at this point in time he was the only family Artemis had. Rosco in his own way befriended Artemis when the two were in the insane asylum. Artemis's father decided long ago to leave. Artemis barely remembered him. Artemis's mother only craved the attention that opium brought her, so when he was stricken by a heavy fever, rather than take him to a hospital, she chose the asylum. His condition was diagnosed as insanity and he was left to rot with all the other mentally ill. Rosco, himself a simpleton, helped Artemis when he could no longer walk, fed him, did the best he could to take care of him, but Rosco could only do so much. Artemis got to a point where he could barely move, slipping in and out of consciousness. Rosco nursed him like a mother would, pouring water into his mouth, even mashing his food so he could get it down. Artemis eventually passed into a coma and even though it looked as if he would die, Rosco remained at his side.

Artemis awoke though, as if by some miracle. Instantly he knew things were different. Everything came to him in an overwhelming wave, thoughts that never before crossed his mind, ideas, concepts. Soon he realized that he couldn't walk, but even with that, he felt more alive than ever. It didn't take long before Artemis came up with a plan of escape and he and Rosco exited the asylum without so much as a whimper from anyone.

Rosco nursed him back to the best of health he could. Artemis tinkered and schemed, drawing schematics and plans that would baffle some of the best scientists in the world. Artemis was on a mission. The fever should have killed him, but instead it made him better. It was clear to him that he received this gift for a reason…a purpose. Artemis would make his mark on the world, a world that treated him like little more than a fly that needed to be swatted. From the day he escaped, he planned to stand up for those who couldn't stand for themselves. That was what his new invention was going to make happen.

The contraption he worked on literally could read the brain waves of any animal or insect. It also could mimic the waves, which allowed Artemis's thoughts to be transferred to whatever wavelength he selected, thus allowing him complete control over whatever animal or insect he chose. This was his gift. Ideas for inventions just came to him and he was able to create them.

The machine he worked on now was actually much more advanced than the one he had tried the night before. This one had no boundaries. Artemis had proven it could make him master over rats as well as hornets.

Rosco came over to him and set down the final piece he needed. He popped the small tube in and hooked power from the battery to it. The tubes glowed and the machine produced a slight humming. Artemis took what appeared to be a special headset, constructed of a metal band and multi-colored wires attached in many places that dropped down to a special power pack that he built into his wheel chair. The headset had two pads made of gold that captured the electrons from his brainwaves and sent them to a small electronic processing device that converted them into an exact match of whatever species he picked.

He began to focus, his copper hued eyes nearly bulging from their sockets. The basement was infested with roaches of all different varieties. It was these creatures which he now focused his attention on. After only a few seconds the insects stopped scurrying and stood stock still. The roaches then began to march in single file from every corner of the basement. They moved with one purpose, their shuffling legs faintly being heard in unison. They crawled up the crates and onto the make shift table. First a couple, but soon there were dozens. They all stood at attention like a well-trained army regiment.

Artemis grinned and chuckled to himself. The chuckle became louder and more pronounced until it was a loud and insane laughter. Rosco soon joined in, even though he had no idea why.

THE TAXICAB CARRYING Fade ground to a halt about a block short of the 42nd Street National Bank. That was as close as he could get. The police had the block surrounding the bank closed off. Fade threw some bills at the driver and exited the cab. His long lanky strides carried him to the scene in no time flat. He immediately flashed his press badge and made his way to where the largest group had gathered, discerning that in all probability this was where the incident had started or ended. Either way it was where he needed to be.

Shock came across his face as he stared at Din standing over what was left of a man, snapping photos. She grimaced with every shot and had to turn her head several times, but she finished and was heading away when Fade approached. He just shook his head as she looked up at him. She winked and blew him a kiss before giving him a smart-assed smirk.

"Well will ya looky here, I guess Mr. Spectacular wasn't able to beat a little old dumb blonde like me over here. I guess maybe I got a few more brains then you give me credit for Mr. Spectacularist."

Fade just grunted as he mumbled under his breath. "Barely." Din pretended not to hear as she started questioning some of the other police officers.

The coroner stood over the body, an inspector beside him. Fade recognized him right away. His name was Perry Brandt, a hard nosed screw who hated all shamuses—Fade more than most. Fade had made him look incompetent on more than a few occasions, so he had earned his notch at the top of the inspector's belt. The inspector was a tall man in his own right, but Fade surpassed him by at least a half a foot. He had dark brown hair that he slicked and combed neatly back under his fedora. He had deep set eyes that appeared to mimic the night sky in their darkness. The cigar that hung loosely at the corner of his mouth fell out completely as his jaw dropped at the sight of Fade approaching. It was followed by a bared teeth grimace and a red shade across his cheeks as he spoke.

"Oh no, Fade. I don't know who the hell let you in here, but this is as far as you go." The inspector moved to shoo him away. Fade stood his ground, holding out his press badge that had been signed by the mayor himself. He was to be granted entrance to any crime scene no matter what—a healthy campaign donation from Hackrox had seen to that. The inspector's shoulders sagged and his face turned even redder as he stepped aside. Fade smirked as he casually walked past the inspector.

"Really, Inspector, I fail to see why you wouldn't want the most capable man on the job anyway." Fade said this with his nose hung in the air and a wry smile on his lips. He first knelt next to what was left of the body. It was a grisly sight, hundreds of jagged grooves where the flesh had been chewed off by rodents' teeth.

Fade looked up at the coroner, who he recognized from previous cases as Nathan Redding. A thin and balding man, his grayish skin tone showed that he didn't get out much. He had dark circles under his eyes, which told of a dedication to what was becoming an overwhelming job of late. The crime rate seemed to rise hourly. This in turn meant the dead bodies were piling up. Redding's office was undermanned.

Fade stood, towering over Redding as he did most everyone. He placed his hand on the coroner's shoulder. "So what have we got here, Nate? It looks like this poor devil was eating alive by...well, hell, by rats."

"Yeah, Fade, it's the damndest thing I've ever seen. This guy looks like he was attacked by half the rats in New York for Christ sakes. I nev'a seen anything like it I tell ya. I mean I 've seen rat bites, but this goes beyond anything that has ever been reported."

Fade dropped his duffle bag and took out a little gizmo from his pocket and ran it over a few spots on the body. It was the size of a cigarette lighter, but in truth it was a battery powered razor of sorts. It would trim areas of material and store them in a container for later research. Redding shook his head as he bent to zip up the body bag, then helped his assistant haul it to the meat wagon.

Fade reached into the dropped duffle bag and removed two things. One was a canister of some white chalky powder, the other a small machine with a lens and a built-in light. First he scattered the powder around the area, and then he turned the lighted machine on and began to look through the lens at the areas the light shined on. He rubbed his chin a few times, deep in thought, saying "Hunh!" as he did so.

Inspector Brandt, having closely monitored Fade's every move up until this point, couldn't help but jump into the mix. Popping a fresh cigar into the corner of his mouth, Brandt bit the end off before bringing a match to it. He puffed on it a few seconds to gather his thoughts. Fade really frosted his lilies, but he was stuck with him until such a time as he could pull the rug out from underneath him. Fade would get his someday, the inspector thought, and then he would get the glory that he deserved. Grinning a little as he walked over to Fade, Brandt was immediately taken back by the sight of the strange device Fade looked through.

"Hey, what the hell is that thing, Fade?"

Fade looked up from the device with a frown. "This is something I came up with to help locate prints…all sorts of prints. See, first I devised this powder mixture, which sticks to oils from not only skin, but soles of shoes as well. Then I shine the special light from this device, which causes the powder to show through this special lens. Here take a look."

Fade reminded Brandt of the typical rogue scholar from high school. The guy that thought everyone was simply beneath him. The inspector nonetheless took the device Fade offered and looked through it. What he saw nearly caused his eyes to bulge from their sockets. There were hundreds, maybe thousands of rat prints all over the gangway as well as the wall.

Fade watched as Brandt gawked at the sight the lens revealed. Fade had already gathered the information he was searching for, so he made his way over to a little opening in the wall about a foot square. Fade found what he was after on the ground below, in the form of a mangled grill that once had covered the hole. Fade had noticed there were prints that ran up and down the wall, to and from this opening. It didn't make sense why the rats would have been in the bank until Fade shined his light in the opening. It was there he noticed one of the wrappers commonly used to hold stacks of currency together. Fade turned his attention to Brandt.

"By any chance," Fade asked, "is there something you're forgetting to tell me?"

Brandt, still marveling at the device Fade had let him look through, scratched his head. "Excuse me, Fade, but why in the hell would I tell ya anything?" Suddenly, the bank manager came running out yelling with his hands raised in the air.

"Robbed, we've been robbed! My God how is it possible?" The man was simply frantic as the Brandt moved over to him to get his statement. Fade smiled to himself, having already figured as much. What he wasn't smiling about was the method by which the bank was robbed. If he was right, someone had figured out a way to control the vermin that lined many of the dank and dirty gutters of New York. The thought made him shudder as he packed up his duffle bag and followed the inspector inside.

Fade followed the manager and Brandt into the bank vault where he heard the manager's anguished tale. He had come in that morning and, despite the scene out back with the body, was preparing to open up. He went through all the normal routines and then on schedule he opened the vault. But unlike most days, this time he received a shock; the vault, though it had been locked, was completely empty of all its cash. The deposit boxes and coins were still intact, but the vault had been holding a hundred and fifty thousand dollars in cash, which was now missing. The frantic manager, now in a full-blown sweat, began to claw at his hair in a mad panic. He just stood there, his jaw hanging open, staring at the empty vault, his head bobbing back and forth in disbelief.

The inspector asked all the normal questions as far as who else had access to the vault and such, but Fade already knew that, Brandt was asking all the wrong things. He walked over to the small one foot by one foot square that matched the one on the outside and shined his light into the shaft. He was sure now more than ever that his theory—as incredible as it sounded—was correct. Trying to keep the inspector from guessing what he found out, he instead reached into his jacket and pulled out a compact case. He clicked a hidden button on the side and three special lenses swung outward, as well as a high-powered light. He moved around the vault casually and spotted the tell-tale signs he sought. Rat hairs. Not wanting to gather Brandt's attention, he quickly hit the button to close up the case, and then deposited it back in his jacket. Fade was not ready to divulge his knowledge to Brandt, wanting instead to have every chance for the *Planet* to bask in the glory of him solving the case.

Fade casually headed for the vault door and exited through it into the bank lobby. Brandt, having caught sight of him exiting, hurried after him.

"Wait up, Fade! You just gonna leave without talking to me?"

"I was hoping," Fade answered. Brandt's jaw dropped a little at first, before becoming a grimace.

"Aw c'mon Fade," Brandt said, his hands outstretched in a questioning pose, "surely you have some ideas about what the hell happened here."

Fade's answer was straight lipped and somewhat callous. "Tons!" Fade continued walking. Brandt thought about hauling his ass down to headquarters, but after a moment thought better of it. He knew it wouldn't get him anywhere except in the mayor's doghouse, besides it wasn't like he shared any of his info with Fade either. Brandt shoved his cigar back in his mouth and headed back into the vault to search for clues.

Fade looked around for Din. He didn't have to look hard, just for the group of officers standing around google eyed, and Din was right dab in the center. He pushed his way through and pulled her aside.

"Listen Peaches, if you can pry yourself away from the crowd of lame gawkers, I need you to get your shots developed and be quick about it. I am not sure if they of course will be of any use, but you must after all earn the overinflated check of yours. Besides, it will make for good eye candy when I wrap this think up."

Din was ready to open her mouth but Fade never gave her a chance as he walked off and hailed a nearby taxi. Din shook her head and stomped her feet. Fade just really rubbed her hard sometimes. A smile, though, came to her face in no time. He was right, she would be well compensated for her efforts. Pulling out a compact and giving herself a once over, she smiled. Closing the compact back up, she headed back to the car that she had been brought in.

WEST EIGHTH STREET was part of Greenwich Village, a quaint little section of town, mostly residential, but with a few businesses and storefronts mixed in. LE-Baulb was just such a storefront. Patrique LeBlanc had opened the small jewelry store over ten years ago and had become quite successful. Patrique wasn't the biggest but he always carried some expensive merchandise, as well as becoming somewhat of a celebrity with all the high priced merchandise and original paintings that dotted the walls. All the upper class and several movie stars were amongst his growing list of clients.

Patrique had just finished up a setting and was putting the jewels in the safe. In the process of getting everything set for closing, Patrique looked forward to a wonderful dinner at one of his favorite restaurants. He was set to lock the safe when he heard the jingle of the little bell that let him know someone had entered the store. He made his way through the heavy curtain that separated his workshop from the front of the store and stepped behind one of the counters. The sight that greeted him was most unwelcome and caused a thin lipped scowl to form on his face.

The sight of a couple of black men greeted him. Patrique was a little startled, but quickly gathered his composure. He was always willing to make new clients, no matter what the variety, but it had been a long day. Besides, they were a couple of strange looking birds. One was emaciated and sat hunched in a wheel chair wearing some sort of strange looking headdress. The other was nearly as wide as he was tall, with a huge head and elongated arms. He appeared to be a solid mound of muscle. He had a strange smile on his face and a strange glint in his eyes, almost seeming crazed.

The pair started toward him. LeBlanq moved from behind the counter with his hands held out as he spoke. "I am sorry, gentlemen, but we are closed, I just have not had a chance to lock up and spin the sign."

Artemis Gray looked up at Patrique with a most sinister smile, his eyes slightly glazed. Patrique caught himself in stride and twirled the edge of his dark Van Dyke nervously.

"I am aware," Artemis spoke in a high pitched and somewhat phlegm choked voice, "that you are not used to folks of our…well our persuasion, entering your small and sheltered world. The world of the rich and well to do…a world that mostly does not include men like us." He paused. "My name is Artemis Gray, sir. Now, whether or not that name becomes one you remember depends largely on how you choose to play your cards over the next few minutes. You see, my good man, simply put we are here to remove your jewels."

Patrique was amazed at the intelligence the man displayed. He didn't know it but Artemis welled with excitement at the vast knowledge that seemed to be in his possession, a welcomed change from the days of being a dullard. "Now don't be alarmed. We only plan on taking a bag full of your merchandise, just a small dent in the fortune you possess."

As if on cue the short man stepped out from behind the wheelchair and held out a burlap sack. Patrique felt his cheeks flush at the prospect of being robbed. Patrique hurriedly stepped from behind the counter as he said, "Now listen here my good man, I will not be plundered like some helpless oaf." With that Patrique moved and grabbed a metal pipe that was concealed next to a case.

The smile on Artemis' face grew larger. It exposed large and somewhat yellowed teeth. Piercing eyes bore into Patrique.

The two men stared at each other for a few moments. As they did, the short man began to slap the burlap sack. A loud buzzing protruded from the bag, causing Patrique to cast his stare at it. Artemis now chuckled, a deep and throaty laugh.

"It is a shame," Artemis said, "you didn't choose to cooperate with me, sir. I am afraid you leave me no choice." With that Artemis raised a hand in gesture and the bag dropped to the floor. As it fell open, a hornet's nest was exposed. Patrique's eyes shot wide with terror as a black and yellow cloud of buzzing whining hornets formed a cloud and hovered at attention, as if awaiting a command.

Patrique looked at Artemis who now had a crazed smile upon his face. He closed his eyes and as if on cue the hornets moved forward and descended upon Patrique, white hot needles bringing their fury to his skin again and again. He tried to run but they enveloped him so that he could barely be seen. It looked like thousands of hornets had formed into a madly waving man. The form moved and then caught the carpet edge and fell through the glass of a display, rolling to the floor and writhing and spitting out choked screams. The movement ended shortly becoming just an occasional twitch, then stopping completely.

The hornets as if on cue left the now lifeless form of Patrique and hovered in the air above him. Artemis again closed his eyes, and as if on cue, the hornets entered the bag where their nest still sat. it took only a short time and they were all neatly back in place, with Roscoe closing the bag back up and tying it off with a rope. The bag was placed on a shelf that was built into the back of the wheel chair. Quickly Roscoe grabbed an empty sack and proceeded to fill it with all the jewels that Artemis pointed out to him. The bag was filled with the finest stuff in no time flat. Rosco tied it closed and placed it in Artemis's lap. The two rolled out of the store as if nothing had transpired.

FADE WAS WORKING away in his lab back at the *Planet*. He sat at a desktop with some sort of radio like device and a soldering iron. Sweat furrowed on his brow, which he impatiently wiped on his shirtsleeve. The device he slaved over was a concept he came up with some time ago that would for a lack of a better word, scramble radio waves. It didn't matter what kind either, the device could gauge whatever sort of wave was being transmitted and then encode a scrambler wave. It was meant to be able to scramble police band waves if a need arose, but with some tinkering… "Yes!" Fade exclaimed to himself.

Fade moved to his large office desk in order to test out the device he just tweaked. He glanced at the glass screen that was built into his desk top. It was yet another of the brilliant devices he devised. It worked off the same concepts of a periscope with mirrors and glass tubes. It allowed him to observe whatever activity was going on outside his office door. This was very helpful indeed for a man who not only made many enemies, but also managed to rub a fair amount of others the wrong way.

Din exited the elevator at that moment, dressed in a scarlet dress from a new design line. She had just come from a massage and felt loose and relaxed. She approached the office door, but before she even knocked there was a click as the lock was disengaged. She pushed the door inward to find Fade sitting behind his desk with his hands crossed together in front of him. He smiled at her, but she knew he was anything but happy. She flung him a half hearted smile and dropped the envelope containing the developed photos she had stopped and picked up on the way up. Fade glanced at the envelope and spoke.

"Well my pampered princess, I hope it wasn't too much trouble taking care of this. I mean it must be rough trying to organize your days, what with all the hair salon appointments, massages, and manicures. But of course, one with limited talents must make the most of what she can." Rising from his seat, Fade walked over to the chair that Din now stood next to. "Here have a seat and take a load off your feet. I mean you must be absolutely exhausted after toughing out another massage from Sven."

"Look here, Mr. Spectacular, get over yourself already. I am here to help if needed and to put into words what the *Planet* pays you the big bucks for. I am not here to put up with your sarcasm or your overinflated ego. I do my job well, and make you look like a genius, and I get paid handsomely for it. The fact that I choose to enjoy life to the fullest, in no way means I have to put up with all your hot air, you got it?" Din stabbed her finger in Fade's chest to emphasize her point, then gave him a Cheshire cat grin and sat down.

"Listen, Din, I have a theory on that bank robbery. I also have a theory on how it was accomplished. I also have an idea on how we might be able to thwart future attempts. If I'm right…hell strike that, I know I'm right, my idea will put a bug in our perp's soup. Here let me show you something." Fade motioned her over to the desk that held the device he had been tinkering with when she walked in. Din shook her head and shot Fade a cocky sneer.

"It looks like a cheap radio Fade, is this your big break through? What are you gonna make the guy beg for mercy by playing bad music over and over?" Fade shot her a dagger filled stare.

"Well Din, I can see where an over-dyed brain like yours would think that way. This however is much more than a simple radio, even though it looks like one. Whoever did that heist at the bank and killed that poor officer, has figured out a way to use electronic waves to get vermin to do his bidding. To speak in terms someone of your intellect can understand, he is able to control lower thought beings, rats in the case of the bank. This device I invented should be able to jam the waves he is using, thereby keeping him from gaining control over the rats, or whatever other thing he tries to control." Fade walked around the desk and turned the device on. There was a little crackling at first and a low humming before the light from its tubes showed through the vents in the side. Fade looked at Din.

"Ok, Din, I need you to walk over to the police band radio in the corner and turn it on please." Din doubted what Fade was saying, but she walked over to the shelf on which sat the police radio and flicked the on switch. There was instant chatter coming from the thing, as it picked up all the calls and communications that New York's finest were sending out. Fade smiled.

"Ok Din, now watch what happens." Fade turned a few dials, and made a few adjustments, and then finally hit a little toggle switch on the front of his device. The chatter that was spewing from the radio instantly became a piercing trill humming, high pitched, and offensive to the hearing. Din winced and brought her hands up to cover her ears. Fade again grinned. He had Din turn the dial to all the different frequencies and channels the police ban covered—the effect was the same on all of them. Satisfied that the device worked, Fade switched the machine off.

Instantly the chatter on the police band started up again as if it had never stopped.

"Din, if my theory is right, this little device should help us to not only get a great story, but in the process, stop a master criminal." Din tilted her head to the side and held her hand up in question. Fade smiled.

Their conversation never came to fruition, as they were interrupted by the ringing of the phone. Din quickly snatched up the receiver and answered it. Her face became a grimace as she listened to the voice on the other end. Hanging up the phone, she relayed to Fade that it was Brandt. There had been another robbery committed in Greenwich Village, with a similar MO. This time it was the owner of a jewelry store. The man had been stung to death, and from appearances, it looked like there had been hundreds of hornets in his little store. Fade shook his head in disgust.

"Din, I want you to listen to my theory on what I think is happening. It is going to sound crazy and far fetched to one such as you." Din rolled her eyes. "But! I am convinced I am on the right path." Fade spent the next twenty minutes explaining his theory to Din while they headed over to the jewelry store. Din was speechless. She had seen some pretty strange stuff while being employed to write Fade's adventures, but this one took the cake.

They arrived at the jewelry store, threw a few bills at the driver, and exited the cab. Fade flashed his *Planet* badge and was allowed to cross the police lines. They walked into the jewelry store and found Brandt and the coroner standing over the lifeless body. As they got a little closer, Din held back a screech by bringing her hand up to her mouth. The body was a gruesome sight with swollen purple lumps covering every inch of the exposed skin. The facial features were unrecognizable. There were dead hornets in every opening, ears, nose, and mouth. Din had to excuse herself to head outside for some fresh air. Brandt seeing Fade, pulled his hat off and ran his fingers through his hair in exasperation as he spoke.

"Fade, I gotta tell ya, I have never seen anything like this. What a horrible way to die." There were no bits of sarcasm as Fade merely nodded in agreement.

"Look, Brandt. I have a reasonable theory I would like to run by you. I don't want you to be intimidated by it, being as how I know it is over you pay grade. I was gonna keep it to myself, but this has to be stopped before another poor fool ends up like this or worse." Brandt ran his cupped hand across his face, trying to keep his composure. This was just Fade's persona, and though Brandt hated it, the ghastly scene before him trumped everything he might feel. Brandt needed to work with Fade and put an end to this as quickly as possible. If that meant eating some crow from Fade, then so be it, this maniac needed to be caught.

Brandt slipped his hat back on and motioned for Fade to follow him. He stopped and whispered a few things to one of the officers standing there and then headed out the front. Fade followed closely behind until they were both standing out front. Brandt spoke first.

"Listen, Fade, I got no love lost for you and I am more than sure the feelings are mutual! But this goes beyond any pettiness we may feel towards each other. There's a coffee shop right up the street, so if you're game we can sit down and lay our cards on the table, and try to work this out."

Fade smirked and shook his head. "I hold the winning hand, Brandt, so follow me and I will explain what needs to be done so even you can understand it." Before Brandt could say anything Fade's long legs had carried him off towards the coffee shop. Brandt felt his blood pressure rise, but calmed and followed Fade to the shop. This was one time he was willing to suffer through Fade's quips to put an end to this madman's scheme.

The two entered the coffee shop and grabbed a booth towards the back. They both ordered just coffee, the sight in the jewelry shop pretty much killed any appetite they might have had. After they ordered Brandt started things off.

"Look, Fade, I understand you're good at what you do, but you have to understand that I have a job to do as well, it may not always be spectacular, but I think I am damn good at what I do. Hell, believe it or not, I may actually have information that you don't know every now and then. So how about losing the mightier-than-thou attitude just this once, ok?" Fade paused as if mulling the thought over and then nodded in agreement. "Ok, so we got what I think is a break on the jewelry store. It sounds crazy, but at this point nothing would shock me. A lady happened to look out of her window around the time we think that the poor fella was killed. But get a loada this. She says she saw a negro in a wheel chair being pushed by another negro who reminded her of an ape, leaving the store right around the time the guy normally closes. She says the two just casually moved down the street and out of sight. Crazy right?"

"Well, Brandt, as you said, right now we don't have much to go on other than my theory. Therefore any clue, however vague, is a plus." Brandt smiled.

"Ok, well lay it on me, Fade, you are if nothing else good for amusement." Brandt chuckled at this but seeing that Fade held a thin lipped and expressionless mouth lost his smirk. "My apologies Fade. Just falling into our usual patterns I guess, by all means please continue."

Fade started to lay out his theory about what was going on, he spared no time, giving out every detail, no matter how minute it might seem. Brandt sat there mesmerized, his mouth hanging open and his eyes not so much as blinking. The theory as far fetched as it sounded seemed to hold water, and even to Brandt, feasible. Brandt took a sip of the coffee that had arrived along with a bite of a complimentary pastry. He wiped the powdered sugar from his chin as he swallowed.

"So basically you're telling me this is like that Pied Piper of Hamlin guy from the fairy tales. Yes?"

Fade nodded half- heartedly as he answered. "Well I guess that's one way of putting it, but yes, I guess in a sense it is. The problem is that, whoever is committing these crimes must possess an intelligence that is off the charts. I mean most living things communicate through sounds and their brains use different sorts of electronic wavelengths to control functions. This man, if he is indeed a man, has figured out not only how to pick up the waves, but to control them." The conversation was interrupted as one of the officers that was on the crime scene burst in through the door. He was short of breath, having apparently sprinted down the street from the jewelry store.

"Inspector…we just got a call that an armored car was hit not far from NYU. One of the guards didn't make it, but the other one managed to survive. But, get this sir, they were attacked by fire ants, you know those ones whose bite feels like someone died a cigarette out on ya. Well anyway the one guard managed to jump in the river so he made it, but just barely. He called it in and described the two Negros to a tee. I guess they took off with the armored car while the guards was busy with the ants."

Brandt was up from his seat with Fade right behind him as they headed back to the jewelry store to get Brandt's car. Brandt instructed the officer to have the descriptions spread around the city. They needed desperately for someone to give them a tip before the mad man struck again. Fade's eyes perked up and he snapped his fingers as a thought jumped into his mind.

"Hey, Brandt. Does NYU still have that large radio transmitter that they were experimenting with? You know? The one that they constructed to send and pick up wavelengths from all over the globe."

Brandt rubbed his chin as he thought about it. "I can't say for sure, Fade, but last I read they were still working on it, trying to reach the stars or something like that. Why, you got something cooking?"

"I think so, listen I have to run back to the *Planet* and get something. I need you to meet me at NYU in about an hour and make sure you get us clearance to use it as well as someone who has worked with it before, or is at least familiar."

Fade was off without waiting for a response. He rushed back to the jewelry store, located Din and then hurried outside the police line to hail a cab. When the cab pulled up he shot him some instructions, herded Din into the backseat, then jumped in beside her. Brandt was close behind and after giving his men some final instructions, jumped in his own car and headed off.

THAT EVENING IN a small warehouse along the East River just down from SOHO, Artemis Gray sat at a makeshift dining table. A candelabra flickered in the middle, casting a shifting light on the spread that Artemis had purchased from one of the finest steakhouses in New York. Rosco sat across from Artemis—his face covered in dripping wine and meat juices. Artemis smiled as he watched Rosco enjoying himself. It had been Rosco who had made it possible for him to survive, and Rosco, who had been his only friend these last few years. No longer need he worry about people throwing racial slurs at him, teasing him, soon every person who had treated them badly would be made to suffer in a cruel and horrible way. The final laugh would be theirs. Artemis chuckled to himself at that thought.

Artemis had rented this place after the bank job, putting down a healthy retainer so no questions or prying eyes would be cast his way. He had big plans for the future and with a few more jobs, he would have all the money he needed for those plans. He took a swig of his fifty year old Bordeaux, swishing it around in his mouth to savor the moment, burying his nose in the glass and sucking in every last bit of the fragrant aroma it cast. He had never come close to anything this sweet in his life and wished to savor every wonderful moment.

Rosco interrupted the moment with a long and pronounced belch. The halfwit obviously approved of Artemis's selection. The sight warmed Artemis's heart and brought a smile to his lips. He chuckled as he spoke.

"That's right, my friend, you enjoy yourself. From this moment on you shall never want for anyhing. You shall never be cast in a dim light. From this moment on, you shall be treated with the compassion and care you showed me these past years ten-fold."

Rosco didn't seem to hear as he dug into another steak and washed it down with another large gulp of wine. Artemis pondered how this halfwit had ever saved him. What great hands of fate had intervened that such a man could save him from the brink of death? It had to be divine efforts that he was granted this reprieve. He was given a gift and it would be a shame … His thoughts were interrupted as Rosco let out another loud and obnoxious belch, following it up with a loud crescendo of farts. Artemis raised his glass in salute. "Excellent my friend." He took a few moments to clear his thoughts before speaking.

"Tonight we enjoy some of the fruits of our labors, for tomorrow we will strike once more my friend. We will bring fear to all those that have ever struck out against us. Artemis Gray will soon be a name spoken in hushed whispers. I will be…unstoppable."

FADE AND DIN made their ways back at the planet. Din was starting to write down some notes for the story she would later print and Fade was putting stuff together to hopefully put an end to the horrible crimes. Of course he would do it in such a way, that he came out looking brilliant and the *Planet* would have yet another 'Spectacular' story.

Fade moved about his lab area in a decisive pace. He walked to one wall and pressed his chin to one chrome strip while reaching down and pressing his left forefinger to another. There was some light whirring as a door seemed to open out of nowhere in the floor. Fade reached in and gathered a few devices he had tinkered with in the past.

The first was an amplifier and several bundles of color coordinated cables. The next was what appeared to be a simple watch. This was far from the truth. Fade in his role as "Crime Spectacularist" had deemed he could solve crime without the use of firearms. This he compensated for with special gadgets that he thought up and had constructed for him. The watch was just such a gadget. He slipped it on his wrist and holding the watch arm in front of him he pushed the top pin in. There was a short swishing sound like a high pressured gas had been released, but only for a second. Fade smiled to himself as he walked over to a world globe that sat on a desk. He ran his hand along it and pulled a small dart from South America mass on the globe. He smiled and shook his head a little as he spoke to himself. "Well I was aiming for the Artic but it was close enough for now."

Fade then placed another gadget that attached to his leg right at the knee. This one he had used many times. It was also a dart gun that was triggered by pressing down a certain way on his right heel. This one usually meant a new pair of trousers would be needed, but as long as he was breathing that was fine. After all he just sent the bill to Hackrox anyway.

Fade walked over to another wall section, this time he pressed against it so both arms were straight out at his sides like the letter 'T'. Again he pressed two of the chrome strips simultaneously and a large wall panel slid open to reveal a hidden closet. It was in here he kept a special lightweight chain mail vest. It cost the *Planet* a fortune, but again it had saved him on more than one occasion by stopping a bullet meant for his heart. He wasn't thinking about bullets this time, but hoped it would keep whatever vermin he might run across from getting at his flesh, giving him every chance he might need to make an escape.

Fade spent the next hour hooking up his wave jammer and amplifier into the *Planet's* own broadcasting equipment and antennae. He then got on the phone to NYU. He had learned from Brandt that a Professor Gregory Sparks was in charge of the radio wave project. He had also learned that there were some issues with funding and therefore the project might be shut down completely.

Fade had a plan but he needed the professor to agree to bring his equipment to the *Plane*t. The professor at first was having none of it, but with some smooth talking, and the promise of the *Planet* making a donation to his project, Fade got his wish. The professor said he could have everything there and hooked up in four hours. Fade hung up the phone. He still had a lot to do and if his plan failed it might be an ugly scene. But he wouldn't dwell on it, it would be running that night, and if he was right it would help to prevent another crime. This was phase one of Fade's plan, but phase two would only be possible if phase one succeeded.

Fade knew that whoever was behind this was a genius. He also knew that this would only thwart him temporarily. That was why he had devised phase two. But no sense in getting ahead of himself, he needed to focus on phase one.

THAT NIGHT SOMETIME after midnight, George O'Reilly, a night watchman at the Manhattan Museum, was making his rounds. The museum wasn't showing any expensive artifacts, so it was just him and Mike Wetzel left on guard duty. That was fine with George. It gave him a chance to hit his flask a little more often and maybe sneak in some shut eye. He was just coming up on a small Chinese display that the museum was getting ready to change when he heard a rustling sound. He pulled out his flashlight and shined it down the hall. The cone of light shined on a sight that made George swear off drinking for the rest of his life.

"Sweet Mother of me ever lovin' Jesus!" he exclaimed. The sight that George was staring at was a Chinese crown and some sort of necklace. That was not the shocking part though; the shocking part was that a group of rats were carrying the items out of the room. They ignored George and scurried down the hall towards the dock area. George shook his head and drew out his .38 service revolver and followed the scurrying rats. It was all he could do to keep up with them.

They rounded a corner, disappearing from his line of vision momentarily. George turned the corner and got a shock. George was now staring into the eyes of two King Cobras. They hissed and swayed to some unseen rhythm, their fangs barred and their tongues flashing in and out.

George leveled his gun to take aim at the one. The other seeming to sense this spit a tar-like substance right in to George's eyes. It burned like the dickens and he lost his vision. His gun dropped to the ground as he himself fell to his knees wailing in agony and feebly trying to wipe the stuff out. It was too late as the snakes were upon him. They took turns striking as George yelped with each strike, flailing his arms blindly at them. Then he could flail no more as he stiffened and fell backward, his breathing labored and raspy before finally stopping all together.

MIKE WETZEL SAT in the guard's office with his feet on the table and the paper folded up in one hand reading the sports page. He looked up at the clock and shook his head. George should have been back awhile ago. Mike swung his feet off the desk and dropped his paper. Standing up, he grabbed a flashlight off the shelf and headed out to see what happened to his partner.

Mike walked down the hall towards the route George would have taking and stopped in his tracks. Staring him in the face were two cobras swaying back and forth. He quickly went for his revolver when the snakes spit at him. Moving quickly Mike was able to ward off the spit, but some of the stuff splashed on his skin and burned like hell, but he could at least see. He tried leveling the revolver but the snakes were already slithering towards him at a rapid pace.

Mike turned to run for the office and was confronted by a horrid sight. Two more cobras blocked the path he had just come from, their heads bobbing up and down, obsidian eyes fixed on him as a target. Mike glanced back at the first snakes and they now stood at attention also. Sweat started to run down Mike's face as he frantically turned from front to back, watching the snakes and trying to figure out a way to save himself. Mike leveled the gun at the ones behind him and was taking aim when the snakes suddenly just dropped and slithered away from him. Turning back he saw that the other two were doing the same thing. Mike didn't wait to question his good fortune, quickly darting into another office and slamming the door behind him. Mike quickly snatched up the phone receiver and dialed police headquarters and asked for a couple of patrol cars. Quickly Mike explained the situation so that they came prepared.

Shortly before in the darkness just outside the museum dock, Artemis and Rosco hid in a van. Artemis ripped the headset from his ears as some loud wailing noise pierced his thought and broke the connection he had with the rats and cobras inside. Artemis cursed out loud in a bitter voice.

"Damn it, Rosco, something is wrong. I need you to get us out of here quickly. That crown the rats were bringing me was from an emperor who ruled during the 16th Dynasty. It was rumored that he had the power to communicate with nature, what a fitting tribute it would have been for me to wear it. But something or someone has figured out a way to jam my headset. Therefore I feel a hasty retreat is in order. I must sit and dwell on how this could have happened."

The van engine roared to life, as Rosco, using the specially designed apparatus Artemis had made for him, sent the van speeding off with a cloud of smoke and screeching tires.

EARLY THE NEXT morning Fade was at the museum, surveying everything that was going on and getting the story firsthand from Mike Wetzel. The poor guy was still shaken up from his run in with the snakes, as well as the news that his friend and partner George had been killed. Mike gave Fade all the details he could while Brandt jotted down notes. Fade formed a grin on his face as the two turned away from the man. Meanwhile, specially trained people from the zoo had tracked down and secured the cobras while the police had either killed or sent the rats scurrying from the museum.

Fade and Brandt exited the museum and stood out front. Brandt was scratching his head as he spoke. "I can't make any sense of what the guy said, Fade. How 'bout you?"

Fade chuckled.

"That's easy, Brandt—I saved the day." Brandt shook his head and rolled his eyes at that comment. Fade catching this said, "Here, let me explain. I had a theory about something and working with the professor at NYU we were able to get his equipment and mine set up at the *Planet*. I started broadcasting the scrambler signal a short time after midnight in the hopes it would show results. It did."

"Ok, so we should have this guy stymied than?" Brandt responded.

"Hardly, Brandt. Whoever this guy is, he has an I.Q. that is well above the Mendosa line. No, I'm afraid it's only a matter of time 'till he figures out a way around my little gimmick. If we are to stop this guy, we need to force his hand. That is where Phase Two of my plan comes in."

Brandt held his hands up in question. "Phase Two?"

"Yes, Brandt. I am going to need your help for this one. I will be heading back to get a headline pushed in to this afternoon's *Planet*. If I'm right it should bring this guy to us, but if not we will need to go back to the drawing board." Fade spent a little time going over his plan detail by detail until he was sure Brandt completely understood. Then he flagged down a taxi and headed back to the Planet.

Once back at the *Planet* he gave Din the headliner he wanted to hit the early edition, then sent her first to Hackrox's office to get his permission and then down to the print room to get the ball rolling. Hackrox of course signed off on it and after a short period, Fade's headline was set to be on the front page of the afternoon copy. Fade sat back in his chair and reached into a drawer pulling out a bottle of fine scotch. He poured himself a glass full and leaned back leisurely taking sips as he contemplated all aspects of his plan. He was satisfied he had covered all the angles pretty well but he didn't know his enemy other than the profile he had figured for him, and the vague descriptions of a few witnesses. It didn't matter at this point, it was too late to turn back, by now the presses were rolling and the papers would hit the street soon.

ARTEMIS SAT ONCE again at his makeshift dining table. He was sipping a glass of Chianti and eating a plate of fettuccini. A stack of newspapers sat on the table next to him. He thumbed through a few before the *Planet* front page came to view. Instantly his glass was banged down, the wine rolling up and over the edge to spill on the table and most of the papers.

The headline read: 'Foster Fade The Crime Spectacularist Solves Vermin Robberies.' In the story, the final line read 'The mayor is to give Fade an award in his office on the fortieth floor of the *Planet* tomorrow night at Eight.'

The last comment caused Artemis to fling the plate of pasta across the table, crashing to the floor and shattering in pieces. Rosco hurried to the spot to clean it up. Then the wine was hurled through the air to shatter against the far wall. Artemis pushed his chair away from the table. Rosco was in a panic. He had never before seen Artemis like this. His simple mind could not fully grasp things, but he knew his friend was very upset, this in turn made Rosco upset, though he was confused as to why.

Artemis headed into the laboratory and rolled his chair up to the table where his device sat. He was beside himself with anger at the headlines he seen in the *Planet*. He screamed aloud, "Fade, I know you not, but you will pay dearly for interfering in my plans. I have been given a special gift and I am the smartest man alive. Your skills are fodder before mine. Do you hear me, Fade?" His whole body shook with rage, then as quickly became calm.

Artemis set to work on his device. There was a curled grin on his face and his eyes seemed to be staring through the device he worked on. It was like his brain was mapping the work out and his hands were following without need of his eyes. Rosco stood and watched unnoticed. He had no comprehension of what was transpiring. He wished only for his friend to be happy.

Rosco finally moved to the small bed he had set up. He knew his friend would be at it all night and would not require his assistance. He laid his head down and was snoring in no time. He dreamed of simple things as simple people do.

The next morning Rosco awoke to his name being reverberated throughout the warehouse. Artemis was obviously in need of him. He rubbed the sleep from his eyes and headed for the lab. He arrived to see Artemis sitting there with the head-set on and a twisted smile and piercing bloodshot eyes. Artemis raised a fist and spoke like a warlord who had conquered some battlefield.

"I've done it, Rosco! I have figured out what this Crime Spectacularist did to interrupt my device. I have taken measures so that this will never happen again." Artemis gave Rosco a very simple list of things he needed and instructions to have the van ready by seven that night. He would again prove his genius by crushing Foster Fade.

FADE HAD THE *Planet* abuzz with activity. He had emptied the place of all but a few police officers disguised as newspaper people. He had all his little gadgets in place including a special set of rubber soled boots he had just finished that day. Now it was just a matter of waiting to see if his bait drew the rat into the trap.

The front desk of the *Planet* was manned by a policeman so when Artemis and Rosco entered the *Planet* followed by a large pack of rats, calmness prevailed. The officer, though packing heat, had no choice but to follow Artemis's instructions as the rats surrounded him from all ends. He calmly directed Artemis to the elevators that would take him up to the fortieth floor. The officer hit a small button along the desk alerting Fade that Artemis was there. It was all he could do, as the rats were left to keep an eye on the lobby.

Fade approached the control panel for his jamming device and flipped a few switches and threw a few buttons. The device hummed into action sending its jamming waves out. Little did he know that they were having no effect on the rats down below. Fade approached his desk and watched the glass screen to await the approach of the madman. He didn't have to wait long before Artemis and Rosco were standing outside his door. Fade was almost in disbelief that a black man in a wheelchair with a black halfwit could accomplish the things they had. He guessed the descriptions were right after all.

Fade took a deep breath and hoped that his plans would pan out. If not, he knew he would be up the proverbial creek without a paddle. He drew a deep breath as he approached the door to greet the man and his lackey. He opened the door and stood straight in front of the wheelchair with his feet spread apart to mimic the width of the chair. The two stared silently for a second and it was in this instance that Fade pushed down on the backs of his heels. In that instance, a small stream of liquid that shot forward from each booth splashing unnoticed on the wheel chair's tires.

Fade stepped back as the lackey wheeled the madman into his office. Fade noticed the headset and the glare of pure hatred in the man's eyes. He moved to a spot so that his foot sat perfectly at the edge of a line patterned in his rug. He spoke then.

"It seems, my friend, that you are quite an inventor. I have however figured out how to thwart your plans."

The man in the wheel chair chuckled unamused, then with a sinister smile he finally spoke. "My dear Mr. Foster Fade—The Crime Spectacularist—you have been as much trouble as a simple gnat that one swats when he becomes annoying, or a roach that one crushes beneath his boot. That is what I am here to do this night—to swat you like the gnat that you are."

Fade wiped some sweat from his forehead. "Well you have me at a disadvantage. You seem to know my name but I have no idea who you are."

The man chuckled again. "What is in a name, Mr. Fade? It will serve you no purpose, but as a—shall we say last request?—I will tell you. I am Artemis Gray, a name that will soon strike fear into every person in this city. My friend is Rosco."

"Well, Artemis, why don't you do yourself a favor and give it up? I am sure the nice men at the padded room hotel will give you and your friend lots of neat stuff to play with."

Artemis just laughed at this notion, a loud and obnoxious laugh. Then he spoke in a cold and drull voice. "I am afraid, Mr. Fade, that your time in the spotlight has come to an end." He raised his hand and snapped his fingers and the lackey jumped out producing a burlap sack which he was intent upon opening. Fade jumped into action, lifting the arm with the wristwatch and pushing the little button. There was a low hiss and Rosco slapped at his neck, pulling the small dart that his probing fingers discovered. This didn't stop him though as he snarled and readied the sack to launch at Fade.

Fade reacted quickly and twisted his right knee a certain way, again there was a light hiss, and again Rosco clawed at his neck. This time though the dart did its job and the man fell to the ground unconscious. The sack upon dropping however, opened enough to expose its content.

Fade stood in momentary shock as he stared face to face with two black mambas. These were two of the deadliest snakes on the planet, and from the looks in their eyes, he was their target. Fade had only one shot, he pushed down on a secret pressure switch that he had lined his foot with. Instantly, special coils of thin wire that were literally weaved into the pattern of the rug were charged with electricity. The snakes hissed and jumped about, before finally writhing no more, unconscious or hopefully…dead.

Fade looked at Artemis and noticed he had a blank stare about him. There was no movement other than some twitching of his cheek muscles. Then the headset began to smoke. Artemis sat there with mouth agape and drool hanging from his lip. It was over. Artemis would never be the same. Foster Fade had triumphed yet again—in spectacular fashion.

THE NEXT DAY, the office had been cleaned up and Fade sat at his desk, tinkering with another gadget. The phone began to ring which brought an instant grimace to his face. "Din!" He shouted. After two more rings and no answer from the platinum blond, Fade muttered some expletives and, setting the gadget down, yanked the receiver from its cradle.

"Fade…wait…hold on a second damnit…it what?" Fade listened, trying to get in a word edgewise. "A million dollars in gold bullion just vanished into thin air from the Reserve. Yup, definitely sounds like something that would be right up my alley Inspector." Fade hung up the phone and rushed out the door. Another spectacular case awaited.

THE END

H. DAVID BLALOCK

GRUDGE MATCH

AN ADVENTURE OF FOSTER FADE
THE CRIME SPECTACULARIST

— I —

FADE IS ACCUSED

THERE IS AN old saying that 3:00 AM is the midnight of the soul.

The *Planet* employees—the inkers and letterers as well as the machinists and deliverymen—had no inkling of the event that would shortly impact them all. The presses at the *Planet* were being prepped for the morning edition when the first explosion happened.

On the fortieth floor of the *Planet* building, Foster Fade was in his apartment suite, dreaming peacefully about his coming fishing trip to the Poconos. Just as he was about to land a record trout, the raucous jangling of his telephone dragged him back to reality. He blinked blearily as he fumbled for the handset, knocking over his alarm clock in the process. The face on the timepiece shattered on impact, further jarring his already raw nerves.

"What is it?" he growled into the phone.

"It's your fault, Fade," a high-pitched, squeaky voice said. "Remember that. Your fault."

The line went dead.

Fade looked at the phone. Had he dreamed that? He jiggled the cradle hook.

"Operator," came the tinny response of a bored voice.

"This is Foster Fade. Did you just route a call to me?"

"Yes, Mr. Fade," the woman said, her voice a little less disinterested.

"Who was it?"

"I'm sorry, Mr. Fade. I didn't ask."

Of course she didn't, he thought. *Why should she?* "Never mind," he mumbled and hung up.

He fished the broken clock off the floor. Its last report had been 3:07. He took one of the slippers by the bed and swept the broken glass under the nightstand. He turned over and went back to sleep.

FADE OVERSLEPT. IT was nearly midmorning before he stuffed his lanky, nearly seven-foot body into the shower. He passed a hand perfunctorily through his perpetually disheveled hair and turned on the radio. The story of the explosions was already circulating, but he wasn't listening too closely. He was going over the checklist for his fishing trip in his head as he washed up. Finally, he headed downstairs for breakfast in the little cafe. It might be a little late for it, but the dolls in the cafe were very accommodating when it came to his little eccentricities.

As usual the lobby was bustling, but he ignored the gawking tourists looking at the huge rotating metal globe that dominated the chamber and the maps of the world spread all on the walls. They were murmuring at the impressive extent of the modernistic architecture. About an hour later, toothpick digging at the remnants of his bacon and eggs, he pressed the button for the elevator and idly watched as the indicator swung down from 30.

"Mr. Fade!"

A boy of about twelve in short trouser pants and sporting a Yankees' baseball cap ran up to him. Fade smiled as the boy skidded to a stop. The little fellow was one of a troop of street gophers working for loose change. Over the last few months, Fade had gotten used to him being underfoot.

"Hello, Tim. What gives?" he asked.

"Two tough looking customers just went up to forty," the boy said breathlessly. "Be careful."

He yanked off the cap, tousled the kid's towhead, then jammed his hat back on. "Thanks, pal. I will. Run some sandwiches up for Din, will ya? Tell 'em to put it on my account. Get one for yourself while you're at it."

Tim smiled broadly. "You betcha, Mr. Fade."

The elevator door opened.

"Good morning, Mr. Fade," the operator droned gruffly. Like all the operators in the building, he was powerfully built. The *Planet* made sure their elevator operators often doubled as company security.

Fade stepped inside, saluting the boy, who scurried off to his task. "Morning," he said absently to the operator.

The doors closed and the room rose in response to the operator's urging.

Fade reached his office to find Dinaminta Stevens sitting at her desk in the outer office with a wry smile. She was a strikingly beautiful lass, a platinum blonde with the voluptuous figure of Mae West and the soft looks of Veronica Lake. Her maroon beret matched the Chanel suit she wore and somehow never wrinkled. It was her pen that made Fade famous with the Crime Spectacularist articles in the *Planet*. In shocking contrast to her looks, her writing was full of violence and gore.

"You been a bad boy, boss?" she asked, raising one pretty eyebrow.

"Not recently that I know of. Why?"

She tilted her head toward the door to his office. "Two detectives waiting in there, and they're unhappy about something."

The *Planet*'s articles on the Crime Spectacularist often depicted the police as all but incompetent. Fade knew this was not going to be pleasant.

"You know, a lot of the reason they hate me has to do with you and your fictions," he needled her.

She batted her eyes innocently. "I just write the truth, Fade. Is it my fault they come off the way they do?"

Fade shook his head. "Call the Marines if I'm not out in five minutes."

He straightened his coat and opened the door to the office.

There wasn't that much difference between them in appearance. Nondescript gray suits, spit-shined wingtips, thin black ties. They stood impatiently with arms crossed, facing the door as he entered.

"Good afternoon, gentlemen," he said to them. "To what do I owe this pleasure?"

"What do you know about the paper mill bombing?" one of them asked.

"Bombing?" Fade repeated as he walked to sit behind his desk.

The other detective dropped a piece of paper on it. "This was delivered to the precinct this morning."

Fade bent forward and looked. It was an article about the Crime Spectacularist and a murder mystery containing bugs and bad guys.

"So?" he asked.

The detective handed him another paper. It was a note made of letters cut from several glossy magazines.

IT'S FADES FAULT. EXPECT MORE. 03121230

Fade looked from the note to the detective. "What's my fault?"

"You tell us. That was found at the paper mill."

Fade leaned back. The telephone call the night before leaped to mind, but he wasn't going to let these flatfoots know. "I don't know anything about it."

The detective leaned on his desk. He smelled of old coffee and gun oil. "Then why does the note say it was your fault?"

"How should I know?" Fade countered, returning the man's glower.

"Look," the policeman said, pointing a finger at him. "If you had anything to do with this you better come clean. It'll go easier for you."

"Why would I blow up a paper mill?" Fade asked, exasperated. "I have reservations at the Poconos for a fishing trip."

"What does it mean by 'expect more'?" the detective pressed.

Fade closed his eyes and sighed. "I already told you, I don't know anything about it."

The detective straightened with a snort. "You just watch it, Mister Crime Spectacularist," he snarled. "We'll be on you like white on rice if we find out you're dirty."

Fade stood. "You've made your point," he said tautly. "Now, I have work to do."

The detective frowned and looked at his fellow, then jerked his head at the door. They left with one last glare at him.

FADE'S OFFICE WAS full of gadgetry but very little of it was obvious to the casual visitor. In the hallways outside, his network of interconnecting gizmos performed sentry duty and provided him a safe avenue of escape in an emergency. The very floor was rigged to deal with intruders, the deep shag rug's disc and bar pattern embedded with enough wiring to make any bad guy dance. Fade had no trouble handling difficult situations. It was difficult people that gave him the most heartburn.

The Honorable Gubb Hackrox, the owner and publisher of the *Planet*, was one of the most difficult people you could ever meet. He peered at Fade from behind his eyeglasses, their ribbon hanging against his fat cheeks. His ample frame threatened to crush the great chair he occupied behind his desk. Hackrox was rumored to have pulled a good five million from the *Planet* even during the Depression. He ran the newspaper through the intimidation and ruthlessness of a hard-nosed businessman. He usually had a soft spot for Fade. After all, it was the Crime Spectacularist stories that sold thousands of extra issues every week. Today, however, his mood was foul toward everyone.

"Don't sit down," he said, growling. "You won't be here that long."

Fade paused halfway into the seat then straightened slowly.

"I got an interesting telegram today," Hackrox barked. He tossed the paper on the desk in front of him. "Read it."

Fade picked up the note.

IT'S FADES FAULT STOP ASK HIM STOP 03121230 STOP

Fade chucked the paper back onto the desk. "I'm getting tired of this," he said.

"You have something to say?"

"All day long people have been showing me messages like that."

The publisher looked unimpressed at the revelation. "All right. I'm asking. What's your fault?" Hackrox scowled.

"How the deuce should I know?"

"What do the numbers mean?" the publisher demanded, thumping the paper with a stubby forefinger.

Fade huffed and waved his arms helplessly. "I don't know!"

"Well, you better find out, Fade. My paper's reputation hangs on your being a straight arrow. If I find out different..." He left the threat unfinished.

"Don't worry. I plan on getting to the bottom of this bucket of clams."

"You better. I've got enough aggravation. I just threw a hack writer out of here. Everybody thinks they're F. Scott Fitzgerald, even elevator operators." Hackrox frowned at him for another moment, then grunted. "Get out."

Fade got.

He was in a dark mood by the time he got back to his office. He stormed through the door.

"Somebody kill your cat?" Din asked from behind her desk.

"I just got read the act by the boss."

Din grinned broadly. "Really? Good for him!"

He scowled at her. "Settle down."

"So, what does Old Gubb want?"

"My soul," Fade complained. "He got a poison pen note with my name on it."

"Oh, that reminds me," she said, pushing some papers around. "I have a telegram for you. Here it is."

Fade unfolded the paper, half suspecting what he would find.

TO FOSTER FADE
FROM AN ADMIRER
03120300 03121230 03130530 03131745 03141200
STOP IT IF YOU CAN STOP

"Who brought this?" he asked, indicating the telegram.

"Western Union," Din answered. "Any ideas?"

He scanned the paper again. "It's like the series of numbers that was on the police note and Hackrox's note." He traced the figures with a forefinger. "What do they mean?"

"Search me," she said. "Telephone numbers?"

"No. Too long."

"Post office boxes? Safety deposit boxes? License tags?"

"Yeah, too many choices. But the sequence must be important." He shook his head. "I'm going in to think."

"Mental lubricant is in the bottom drawer."

"God bless the repeal," Fade said.

He shouldered his way into the office and thumped down behind the desk with a sigh. He idly noticed the time as he leaned back.

Half past twelve.

Abruptly the building shook and a rumble brought him out from behind the desk. He darted into the reception area and found Din against the wall, her face pale as her platinum coiffure.

"Fade?" she quavered.

"Steady," he told her, grabbing her by the shoulders. "Are you hurt?"

"I was going to get some coffee and must have tripped over my own stupid feet," she said with a weak smile. "Bumped my noggin on the wall as I went down. I'll be fine."

"Let's get you into the office," he said, lifting her off the floor.

"Really, I'll be okay," she objected.

"You just let Papa Fade be the judge of that, hussy. Now, come on."

He led her into his office, not noticing the figure standing just outside the elevator, watching.

— 2 —
THE BOMBS HEAT UP

THE LOBBY WAS a shambles. The revolving door hung askew while the glass in it and the other doors lay in shards everywhere. The impact of the blast had jammed the clockwork of the huge rotating metal globe, bringing it to a halt for the first time since the *Planet* first went to press. The bomb victims, tourists and employees alike, lay broken as police and firemen went about doing what they could to bring relief while a steady stream of screeching ambulances roared to and fro in the avenue. Smoke hung thickly in the air.

Fade picked his way through the crowd, pausing when he noticed a small body covered with a sheet beside two others. He knelt down beside it and pulled back the cover.

A battered Yankees ball cap tumbled out of the folds of the sheet. It was Tim. The boy must have been hit by falling debris. Fade clenched his teeth and turned his head from the sight as he replaced the cover. Sick to his stomach, he stumbled into the street, dodging rubbernecking taxis. He reached the other side of the avenue and turned to look back.

The little gift shop next to the *Planet* was destroyed. Rubble from the shop was strewn into the street and sidewalk. Smoke poured from its remains. Windows had broken on all the buildings around it up to the third floor. Bits of ornamental brickwork had dislodged and burst against the pavement. He whistled and shook his head. It had been a dickens of a blast for him to feel it all the way up on the fortieth floor.

"Some mess, huh?"

It was Din. She must have come up beside him while an ambulance wailed off because Fade hadn't heard her approach.

"Yeah," he replied, watching yet another ambulance leave. He coughed as dust kicked up from its departure.

"I hear several people died."

"Yeah. Tim was one," Fade mumbled.

Din gasped, hand flying to her face. "Tim? My God."

"Whoever is doing this is one heartless..." He choked off the word. Another ambulance pulled away as he turned toward Din.

"You figure the police will think you know something about this?" Din asked.

"What do you mean?"

"Well," Din said, "it did happen near the *Planet*."

"That means nothing," Fade said, waving that away.

"They might think so."

Fade didn't respond. The loss of life and property was bad enough, but the way the police were acting combined with the accusatory notes made it look more and more like he was being made a patsy for somebody's devilish game. This was definitely personal now, whether the bomber had intended that or not.

But who was he?

THE OFFICES OF Bryan Manufacturing were empty as dawn rose. A large maker of printing machines in the state of New York, their biggest client was the *Planet*, although they also provided jobbing presses for local businesses. Located in Brooklyn, Bryan Manufacturing had been in business about ten years. People were beginning to arrive for the day's duty when the clock on the wall of the supply room ticked over to 5:30 AM.

The blast killed or at least deafened anyone within a half mile and Bryan Manufacturing was no more. The fireball climbed nearly one hundred feet into the air, the explosion sending parts of the building raining down into the surrounding area. Police and fire trucks began arriving within minutes but all they could do was watch the place burn to the ground.

Standing in the cover of a building just down the road, a dark figure watched the authorities in their futile efforts. He smiled and slipped away into the murk.

FADE MANEUVERED THROUGH the workers busy at repairing the damage to the *Planet* lobby, thinking about the radio report of the explosion at Bryan Manufacturing earlier. The *Planet's* stringers had picked up on it within an hour of the bombing and relayed the information for a rush second morning edition, but even so the radio somehow nearly scooped them. He chewed on a doughnut as he pushed the call button for the elevator and watched the repairmen work as he waited for the car to arrive. He was very glad they could still be working. The *Planet* had been lucky. The building was well built and stood up to the blast fine. The building on the other side of the gift shop hadn't been so lucky. It was being prepared for demolition.

The elevator arrived and Fade stepped in.

"Forty," he told the operator.

"Yes sir, Mr. Fade."

As they rode in silence, Fade turned over the events of the last few hours in his head. The paper mill bombing, then near the *Planet* tower, then Bryan's this morning. What was the connection between the telegrams and the bombings? There had to be one, but exactly how?

Fade stepped out on the fortieth floor. Din stood as he walked toward the office door.

"Hi, Fade. Got something for you." She handed him an envelope. "Another telegram. It came just an hour ago. The telegraph office said it came from a station in Yonkers."

He thumbed it open and unfolded the message.

POLICE WONT HELP STOP 03131745 STOP

He stared at the numbers. A sudden thought hit him.

"What's today?"

"Tuesday, why?"

"The date. What's the date?"

"March 13th."

He snapped his fingers. "March 13th. 0313." He looked at his pocket watch. "It's just after 9:00. That means we have less than nine hours."

"Until what?"

"Until the next bomb goes off," he said. "Grab your coat. We're heading to Yonkers to talk to that telegraph office."

THE YONKERS OFFICE was close enough to the Hudson River to smell it. Fade and Din arrived just before 11:00 to find the place already busy with lunchtime customers. Luckily, all three people in line recognized him and didn't object when he asked to step up to the window ahead of them.

"Can I help you?" the woman behind the counter asked, eying him with interest. She was in her early twenties, sporting one of the new natural hairstyles. She tugged at a curl in the back and said, "Say, aren't you Foster Fade?"

"That I am, my dear..." Fade said, smiling as charmingly as he could.

"Kathy," she said, returning the smile.

"Kathy. I was wondering if you could tell me who sent this telegram to me? I'm afraid they neglected to sign it. As you can see, it seems to be rather urgent."

She took the offered telegram and quickly read it. "I don't recognize the message. Let me check the night man's log."

"Thanks very much."

With another smile, she disappeared. Fade took the few minutes she was gone to exchange some words with the others in the office, answering questions about his past exploits that oft times he could not recall. Luckily, Din was there to "remind" him of this or that detail.

"Mr. Fade, I have the order here," Kathy finally said from the counter. She handed the paperwork to him. "I'm afraid the telegram was transcribed from a note slipped under the door during the night with cash payment, so no one, not even the night watchman, saw who left it. I'm terribly sorry."

Fade hid his disappointment behind a grin. "Thanks anyway, Kathy."

"I get off at 5:00," she told him with a sidewise glance, passing a folded piece of paper to him. "Call me."

A slim hand appeared on Fade's shoulder from behind.

"Sorry, honey," Din said, pulling Fade away. She shot the other woman a cold smile. "He's busy."

While Kathy sulked, Fade let himself be ushered out of the building and hustled into his car. As they wove their way through traffic back to his office, he considered the situation.

He was a cagey one, this bomber. A blasted ghost. Worse, if the numbers were any indication, there was more to come. Much more. He had to crack this or more people would die. Well, he wasn't going to just let that happen. He was going to do everything in his power to stop the killing.

They arrived back at the *Planet* at half past noon. He was acutely aware of the time passing all too quickly. They hardly had time to think about what to do next when the telephone rang, nearly making him jump.

"Fade," he said into the receiver.

"Hello, Crime Spectacularist," the voice on the other end squeaked snidely. Obviously, the person was trying to disguise their voice. "I see you solved part of the riddle."

It was the same voice from the late night call.

"Who is this?" he demanded. He pressed a button in his desk. The button sent a signal to the operator to trace the call. The switchboard would recognize the signal and set the wheels in motion. He just needed to keep the line open long enough.

"You don't know me," came the reply. "Not yet, but you will."

"What do you want?" he asked.

"What do I want?" the caller said with a chuckle. "Just to prove you're not as smart as you think you are."

"Why?"

"Let's just say, I have a score to settle."

"What score?"

"Check your messages."

The line went dead. Fade waited on the line for the report from the operator.

"Hello," the operator's voice came on. "We traced the call to a public telephone in Yonkers."

A public phone? And Yonkers again.

"Do you have any messages for me?" he asked.

"Just a moment." There was a slight delay as the operator located the note. "Yes, just one. It says 'Central Park'."

"That's all?"

"Yes, Mr. Fade."

He thanked the operator and hung up. He pulled out his watch. 12:45. The clock was ticking. What did the message mean? The location of the next bomb? Or was it just a red herring? He couldn't afford to ignore the chance it might be the next target.

Best to get there and take a look around. He headed out of the office.

"What's up?" Din asked as he went by.

"Going out."

"Wait, I'll go with you," she said, reaching for her pad and camera.

"I don't know about that. I may get in trouble."

"Good. I need a new Crime Spectacularist article."

"You may get more than you bargain for," Fade warned.

"Shut up and get going."

CENTRAL PARK WAS a large patch of green in the middle of the steel and concrete that was New York City. Although the park itself was pretty overgrown and sheep grazed in its meadows, there were areas still relatively clean where people walked and picnicked on multicolored blankets. People sat on benches feeding pigeons and little kids played ball. It was a glorious spring day.

Fade paid the taxicab and walked with Din into the park, glancing at his watch. 1:30. About four hours to go. Maybe. He looked around. It had never dawned on him how big the park was until now. If there was a bomb, how would he find it in time?

A beat copper walked by, whistling. He resisted the urge to ask the man if he had seen anything out of the ordinary. No sense in causing trouble just yet.

"We better split up," he told Din. "You head that way. Meet me back here in an hour."

"What if I find something?"

"Don't touch anything and come get me here in an hour," he repeated. "We should have enough time."

Din looked uncertain. "Shouldn't I tell the cop?"

"Do you want a story or not? If you tell a cop, that's the end of that."

She nodded. "An hour." She headed off, giving him one quick look back before turning to her search.

He made his way through the park, alert for anything that might look odd or out of place. He paused to watch some children playing with their dog. A sick feeling settled on his stomach to think what might happen.

"You're Foster Fade, aren't you?"

He spun to find himself facing a young smiling couple carrying an infant.

"You are!" the woman said, excited. "I recognize you from your picture in the paper. Could we have your autograph?"

The man offered him a pencil and a memo pad. Fade took it, smiling best he could, and scribbled his name.

— 3 —
FADE MAKES A CHOICE

SOMEBODY WAS POUNDING on the inside of his head. He painfully opened his eyes. Several people were standing around him with concern written on their faces. Din knelt beside him, stroking his forehead. Fade recognized the young couple he met earlier standing behind her.

"You okay?" she asked.

He struggled to sit up, holding his head to keep it from falling off.

"I saw it all," the young man said. "The other guy ran off with the case."

Fade blinked away the spots. "I'm okay. Just got my bell rung."

"What's all this?"

The policeman shouldered his way through the crowd. He stopped over Fade.

"You okay, buddy?" the cop asked.

"That's Foster Fade, the Crime Spectacularist," the young lady with the baby informed.

"Well, well, so it is." The cop turned to the others. "Okay, okay, show's over. Everybody go back to your business." He began shooing the rubberneckers off.

Fade got unsteadily to his feet. "Hang on, Officer, I want to talk to them." He pointed at the young couple.

"All right, but the rest of youse move along."

Fade rubbed his aching neck. "What's your name?"

"Robert Mulligan," the man said. "This is my wife Anne and my son Bobby."

"Pleased to meet you, Robert, Anne. This is Din Stevens."

"Charmed," Din said with a smile.

Fade reached for his pocket watch. It was missing. "Anyone have the time?"

"About a quarter past two. Why?" Mulligan said.

Fade breathed a sigh of relief. "Which way did the man go?"

"He left the park. I saw him get into a taxi."

"Did you notice the company?"

"Better than that," Mulligan said with a satisfied smirk. "I got its number."

Fade reached out and shook the man's hand. "You have no idea how helpful you've been, Robert. You may just have saved hundreds of lives."

Both Mulligans smiled in stunned disbelief.

"Really? Gosh!" Anne said.

"Now, what was that number?"

THE TAXI COMPANY dispatcher said they dropped the fare at an address in Yonkers. Fade wasn't surprised at that. He *was* surprised to find a message waiting for him in his office. Another telegram.

YOU DIDNT THINK IT WOULD BE THAT EASY DID YOU STOP 03131745 STOP BEDLOES ISLAND STOP IT IF YOU CAN STOP

Fade folded the message and grimaced. He was getting annoyed at being pushed around like a pawn, but there wasn't much choice. He reached into the box of cigarettes on his desk and took two out. Although he never smoked, he placed them in a silver cigarette case and tucked them into an inside coat pocket. He walked to the wall and simultaneously pressed two of the shiny metal strips set in the panels. A section of the wall opened to reveal a closet containing several changes of clothing. He reached into a heavy coat and pulled out a roll of cloth tied with a leather thong. This he placed in his pants pocket.

He was ready. Walking into the reception area, he tapped on Din's desk. She looked up from shining her nails.

"Want to see the Statue of Liberty?" he asked her.

"I thought you'd never ask."

"Get your gear."

NEW YORK HARBOR was always busy. An airship buzzed overhead, bound for Lakehurst. Marine traffic carried on twenty four hours a day, but the ferry to Bedloe's Island sat idle at the wharf while Fade and Din walked about the walls of the old Fort Wood. Din carried a camera case. "To document the Crime Spectacularist in action," she said.

"What time is it?" he asked Din after they had been completely around the island once.

"A quarter to four," she told him. She sat down on one of the concrete rails and took off her shoe to rub her foot. "It's not here, Fade. Let's just go."

He shook his head, pacing toward the beach. "There's something here, something the bomber wants me to see."

"Like what?"

Something in the surf caught his eye.

"Like that," he said.

It was a body, a man dressed in tweed. The water lapped over the face, but the bullet hole between the man's eyes was distinctly visible. Din hobbled over to look, then stifled a gasp.

"Is that him?" she asked.

"It looks like the same man," Fade admitted.

"Well, he's not much of a threat anymore," she observed.

Fade scrambled down the steep embankment to the body. He searched the coat and pants pockets. Nothing. No wallet, no watch. He settled back on his haunches and thought. The man must have brought the satchel to the island, whereupon the real bomber shot him. Obviously the man was just a distraction to confuse Fade. But why involve this man at all? Was he an accomplice? A partner?

He flipped the coat open. Underneath, the man's clothes were threadbare. His shoes had holes in the bottoms. He had a piece of rope for a belt.

"I don't think this one was ever much of a threat," he called up to Din. "He's just a hobo."

"That means the bomber's still out there," Din answered.

"So is the bomb." He stood and climbed back up beside her.

"Is this why he wanted you to come here? To find the body?"

Fade shook his head. "Remember the numbers. He's taunting me.

We need to search again."

"And if we find the bomb? What then?"

"We defuse it."

Din sighed. "I was afraid you'd say that."

IT WAS 4:30 when they found it, hidden in a little alcove camouflaged against the very walls of the old fort.

Fade pulled the satchel out and carried it away from the public area. He set it on the ground. He produced the leather-bound cloth roll from his pocket and untied the cord. It unrolled into a small toolkit consisting of a little screwdriver, a tiny pair of gas pliers, scissors, a folded hacksaw with several blades, and a knife.

"You might want to stand clear," he advised Din.

"What, and miss the fun?" She shook her head. She unloaded her camera and set it up. "I can see the headline now. 'Crime Spectacularist Defuses Bomb'. Great stuff."

"Suit yourself," Fade shrugged. "Can't say I didn't warn you."

He examined the satchel closely. There was no telltale ticking of a timing device, but he knew it had to have a detonator of some kind. What kind of timed bomb could it be?

He read recently about a device that used a capacitor to control the timing and detonation of a bomb. It took the place of the plunger generator or clock timer. It had the advantage of stealth, as it didn't give off any noise. The capacitor was put into a small electrical circuit connected to a battery. When it was fully charged it would discharge suddenly, causing a surge and detonating the bomb. If this was that kind of device...

The bag opened at the top, so he concentrated first on the locking straps. They snapped open easily and he warily pushed them back. He inserted the knife blade into the closed mouth of the bag and ran it very gently from one end to another. There was no resistance.

He slowly pulled the bag open. Inside was a metal box with two buttons on its cover. Fade reached in and carefully lifted the box out of the bag. He felt a slight tug and stopped cold. A drop of sweat tickled the end of his nose.

"Din."

"Yeah?"

"I think there's a wire under the box. Have a look inside, will you?"

The blonde peeked in and whistled.

"What?" Fade asked.

"There must be six or seven sticks of dynamite in there."

"Hell," Fade growled. "Can you see the blasting cap?"

"Nope. All I can see is the dynamite."

He lowered the box back into the bag and settled back to consider his next move.

"What about cutting out the bottom?" Din suggested.

"Leather's too thick. I don't think we have enough time."

Din looked at her watch. "It's twenty until five. We have about an hour, if you're right."

"I'd rather not run right up to the wire, if you don't mind."

Din sat down beside him. "What about the buttons?"

They looked at the box. The buttons were exactly alike and spaced evenly between the edge of the box and each other.

"What do you figure?" she asked.

"A test," Fade determined. "One disarms, one detonates. A test of how smart or how brave I am."

"Well, it's fifty-fifty with the buttons or we chance cutting off the bottom in time."

"Not much of a choice," Fade said.

He looked again at the buttons. Why the test? Anybody could have stumbled onto the bag and opened it. The bomber couldn't have known who would have done it. He could have let the police do it. How would that have served to settle his score?

He reached in and pressed a button.

Din jumped back with a yelp. "Are you nuts?" she screamed.

Nothing happened. She leaned back in, but shrieked and fell back again when Fade pushed the other button.

"You're certifiable!" she scolded.

Fade laughed. "The buttons are dummies. It occurred to me this guy wants me to suffer. He wants to show he's smarter than me, so why blow me up? He wants to humiliate me, and he can't humiliate a dead man."

"Well you could have said something!"

"Sorry about that. Anyway, this bomb is still live."

Din started. "I thought you said it was a dummy."

"I said the *buttons* were dummies." He reached into the bag and pulled out the box. He yanked the wires out and tossed the box to Din.

"There you go. A souvenir." He peered into the bag. The dynamite sticks were bound with black tape. He gingerly wrapped his fingers around them and yelped when he felt something sting him. "Found the battery." He shifted his hand. "I think I can get the whole thing out." He proceeded to lift the entire bomb out of the bag and turned it over. There was no obvious timer, just a small metal can and two little bug like things, all connected by wires to each other. Fade set it down gently and picked up his scissors.

"You sure you know what you're doing?" Din asked.

"A little late to ask," Fade said, not looking up from his task. "You still have time to get clear."

"Just get on with it."

He knew he couldn't chance cutting anything near the battery. That could cause the capacitor to discharge and blow them both sky high. From what he read he guessed the capacitor was the metal can with the leads coming out of its top. He placed the scissors on the wire from the capacitor to the blasting cap. He looked at Din.

"Ready?"

Din nodded.

Fade cut the wire.

— 4 —
FADE TAKES A RIDE

FADE'S CONVERTIBLE ROARED to a stop at the Yonkers address the taxi company had given him. The neighborhood was showing its age and the house he stepped up to had peeling paint and cracked windows. Fade peered through the windows and knocked on the door in vain. The place looked deserted. He reached into his pocket and took out his lock picks. In a matter of seconds the door surrendered and he was inside.

The furniture draperies were dusty and yellowed. Each step left a footprint on the floor, but his weren't the only ones. There had been traffic through these rooms, and recently. The footprints led to the back through the kitchen and up to the basement door. Fade pressed an ear to it but heard nothing. He turned the knob and opened the door a crack to peek around it. A darkened staircase led downward. He paused and listened again. Hearing nothing, he opened the door completely and searched for an electric light switch. He found it and twisted it on, flooding the basement with light from two bare bulbs.

There was no mistaking what the basement was used for. It was here the bombs were made. Electrical material, blasting caps, tools, even a box labeled High Explosives were scattered about. Fade poked about the room until his eyes rested on an envelope on the largest workbench. He picked it up.

It was addressed to the Crime Spectacularist.

Hello, Mr. Crime Spectacularist,

I don't want it to end just yet, so this is to let you know you have ten minutes from the time the lights came on.

An Admirer

Fade only took the time to tuck the letter into his pocket then shot upstairs and out of the building. The explosion obliterated the house with a blast that shattered windows for three blocks. The concussion threw him into the street and nearly knocked him out. He was just able to scramble out of the way of a passing car, too deafened to hear its blaring horn and squealing brakes.

He sat down on the sidewalk.

It had been a heck of a day.

BACK IN HIS office, he sat with Din and went over what they knew.

"The bomber finally made a mistake," Fade told her. "He left me a note."

"So?"

"All his other messages to me were by telegram. This one is typewritten."

Din looked at the paper. "I don't get it. How does that help?" she asked.

"Every typewriter has a standard set of print heads, but over time they wear. Eventually you get letters with incomplete or filled loops. This one is new. The letters are crisp and clean. That means it was recently purchased."

"So we check for typewriter sales in Yonkers for the last, what, month?" she ventured.

"Right. He probably bought it the same time he got the rest of his stuff."

"And there can't have been that many people buying bomb making materials in the last month."

"Off to the telephone with you, hussy!" Fade said. "Let's find out who has."

The next few hours went by quickly, but Fade couldn't put one detail out of his mind: the last set of numbers in that telegram. 03141200. They only had until noon to solve this mystery. Would the bombings stop then? Or would they get another telegram? He had to solve this before that next bomb went off.

"Got it!" Din shouted in triumph as she brought him a memo pad filled with numbers. "A man fitting the same description bought supplies at a hardware store and from a demolitions warehouse two weeks ago.

The owners remembered him because he had a scar on his left cheek and a tattoo of an anchor on his arm."

Fade frowned. "I hope that's not another decoy."

"I hadn't thought of that," Din said, deflating a bit. "But you know, the description seems awfully familiar."

"How's that?"

She snapped her fingers. "The elevator operator!"

"Who?"

"The mug who runs the elevator nearest the office. That's who I'm reminded of."

Fade looked sideways at her. "The elevator operator?"

She nodded. "His name is Mark... something." She clenched her teeth and rubbed her forehead. "What was it? Mark..."

"We can find his name in the company payroll records," Fade pointed out. He made for the door. "Or, we can take the direct approach."

"It's already 10:30," Din told him, hurrying after.

They ran down the hallway to call the elevator. Fade watched the pointer above the door as it rose toward 40. It could be he was going to finally meet his tormentor face to face.

The elevator reached their floor and the doors opened to reveal a man of about 30 years dressed in an operator's uniform. He had a scar on his left cheek and Fade was sure there would be a tattoo of an anchor on his arm.

"Floor please," the man said in a bored tone.

Fade and Din stepped into the car.

"Mark?" Fade addressed the man.

The operator started. "Yes, Mr. Fade?"

"Would you mind showing me your arms?"

The operator stood uncertainly looking at them for a moment. Then a gun suddenly appeared in his hand, pointed at them.

"So, you finally figured it out," he said with a sneer. "Took you long enough."

"Yeah," Fade said. "What now? Shoot us here? You wouldn't get out of the building."

The elevator call bell rang. Mark closed the doors without taking his eyes off Fade and Din.

"Oh, I'll get out all right. Don't worry about me. I have a bomb all ready to eliminate any evidence of my involvement and take care of the Crime Spectacularist at the same time. We'll take a little ride to Yonkers where you can enjoy your last few minutes, Fade."

"If you mean that house with the booby trapped basement, I've already been there," Fade revealed. "I'm afraid there's not much left of it."

Mark frowned and grit his teeth. "Damn. Never mind. We're still taking that ride."

"Look forward to it," Fade told the operator with a grimace. "So, mind if I have at least one last smoke?"

The villain laughed. "Want a blindfold too?"

Fade shook his head. He reached for the cigarette case, pausing when Mark hissed and his hand tightened on the weapon. Fade opened his coat to show he wasn't armed. "Just a smoke will do."

"Get on with it, then."

"I have to hand it to you," Fade said as he took out the silver cigarette case and drew a cigarette from it. "You've been hard to find."

"And I was right under your nose the whole time," the operator smirked.

"Before you kill us, why did you kill the hobo? Was he your partner?"

"Partner?" Mark laughed as he pushed the control to lower the car. "I gave him a fin to go to Central Park with the bomb to lure you to Bedloe's Island. The fool bungled it and then he wanted more money, so I took care of him."

"Why did you want to lure me to Bedloe's?"

"To see how you did with the bomb, of course. After all, I needed to know how much you knew about the design."

"What difference would that make?"

"It would make a great detail for the story I'm writing. 'The Last Case of the Crime Spectacularist'. Has a great ring to it, don't it?"

Fade stared at the man. "All this was for a story? You killed people, blew up buildings, for a story?"

"Great stories require sacrifice. Blood and sex sells. You should know that."

The Crime Spectacularist shook his head. "That may be, but why me? What do you have against me personally?"

"I spent six months working on articles about Capone, right up to him being sent up. Took 'em to Hackrox and told him I'd let him use 'em for a song. You know what he told me? 'Capone is old news'. Old news? The biggest boss in history? Old News? 'Besides,' he said, 'we have the Crime Spectacularist.'" The operator waved the gun at

Fade menacingly. "Without the Crime Spectacularist, the *Planet*'s just another rag. Hackrox shouldn't have turned me down. Pretty soon he'll know that. You'll be dead, the *Planet*'ll be scooped on your last case, and Hackrox'll be small potatoes."

The elevator reached the lobby and the operator stopped the car. Mark motioned them outside. "Just keep quiet and nobody else'll get hurt."

Fade smiled grimly. He raised the cigarette to his lips, surreptitiously crushing the slim vial of sleeping gas inside its tube. He blew the gas into the operator's face, holding his own breath.

The man's face went instantly slack and he collapsed without another sound. After recovering the gun, Fade reached over the fallen form and cranked open the elevator doors. There was a sound behind him as the gas cleared. He spun, bringing the commandeered weapon to bear.

Din was sinking to the floor of the car, whether from the gas or the excitement. Fade grinned at her and shook his head.

"Sweet dreams," he told her.

The people outside the elevator stood gaping at him. He grinned at them as they scurried away like startled pigeons. He couldn't help but chuckle when he thought about what they would be telling the police. The elevator operator and a real looker of a dame conked out on the floor of the elevator and a mad looking seven foot tall skeleton standing over them.

Oh well, the mystery was solved. He settled down beside Din to wait for the coppers. As he did, Din mumbled something and started to sit up.

"Have a nice nap?" he asked her.

She gasped and grabbed his arm. "Mark?"

Fade motioned at the unconscious operator. "Still out."

"Thank goodness." She adjusted her hat. "Well, now what?"

He wondered if he could salvage his reservations. "I'll babysit our friend here. Get me a cuppa joe, will ya?"

Din gave him a dirty look then left, shouldering her way through the crowd. A few minutes later she returned with two policemen in tow. A shortish, bespectacled man in a tweed suit brought up the end of the train. Din stood back to watch as the cops dragged the semiconscious man away.

"Where's my coffee?" Fade asked, feigning irritation.

"Still in the pot," she replied. She indicated the little gentleman at her side. "Fade, this is Mr. Stoker."

Fade frowned at her. "Yeah? Nice to meet you." He offered his hand.

"I sincerely hope you can help me, Mr. Fade," Stoker said in a reedy, breathy voice.

"What's the problem?"

"Well," the man coughed and lowered his voice. "You see, I'm an electrical engineer. I have been working with the Army Air Corps on a new process for targeting and..."

"Go on."

"I'm pretty sure if you can't help me, I'm going to be murdered."

Fade sighed. "Mr. Stoker, wouldn't it be more appropriate to take this up with your superiors?"

The man shook his head firmly. "Absolutely not!"

"What makes you think so?" Fade asked.

The other reached into his suit pocket and produced several folded sheets of paper. He handed them to Fade. Unfolding them, Fade found each contained death threats constructed from letters and words cut from newspapers and magazines.

Each of the notes was on U.S. War Department letterhead.

He refolded the notes.

"Well, Mr. Stoker, let's go up to my office to discuss this, shall we?"

THE END

ADAM LANCE GARCIA

THE BLACK ROCK CONSPIRACY

AN ADVENTURE OF FOSTER FADE
THE CRIME SPECTACULARIST

Chapter 1
FACES ON THE TRAIN

THE MOON SHIMMERED in the haze of midnight, the stars barely visible behind grey clouds and the Three Hills. Heavy breaths and panicked footfalls echoed through the town. Somewhere a door burst open, a coin dropped and a rotary dial turned.

"Foster... Foster, it's me. Foster, are you there?"

There was a short electronic sizzle on the other end of the line, followed quickly by the crackling voice of the Crime Spectacularist. "Hello, this is Foster Fade, and you are listening to an experiment in telephone message recordings, using a number of magnetic tapes and a few other—it would take too long to explain. Either way, I'm not currently available to take your call, but if you leave your name, number and a brief message after the tone, you will help advance communication into the next century! Thank you! ...Now, Din press that button over—"

The caller leaned his sweating brow against the wall. It was over. He waited for the tone to sound.

"Foster. It's all true. Every word of it. I know it sounds impossible but they did it. I saw it with my own eyes..." The caller let out a stuttering breath. "But, they found me and there's no coming back from this, ol' buddy. Just make sure you—"

The line went dead.

The police found the body six days later, sprawled out on the bed of an abandoned cabin atop South Grand. There had been no sign of a struggle, no manner of bruising or injury to the body save for a single puncture wound just behind the left ear. They called Fade up to identify the body. Fade had stared at the cold form for several minutes with glass eyes before he simply nodded in uncharacteristic silence. Officially, the cause of death was listed as a heart attack and the case was marked "solved" before it was sealed up, stashed away, and forgotten under dust.

But as the years ticked by, Foster Fade never forgot, not once, listening to the message over and over until he nearly wore off the magnetic strip, the voice recording becoming more and more distant with time, but always reverberating in Fade's mind.

He knew the killer was out there. He just needed to find the right bait…

THE CONDUCTOR GRIPPED the back of a seat as he called out their arrival at Poughkeepsie Station. The brakes squealed and the world outside slowed to a stop. Travel worn passengers filed into the aisle and out onto the platform, leaving the car sparsely populated. Despite a few fresh faces, only a handful of riders remained for the trip back to New York City.

"Grand Central Station, next!" the conductor shouted as the train pulled away from Poughkeepsie, his voice echoing in the near empty car. The setting sun stuttered through the windows with increasing rhythm. "New York City next!"

"George," an older woman whispered excitedly to her husband, tugging at his coat sleeve as they took their seats. "George… Do you think that's him?"

Her husband looked over to the tall redheaded man sleeping in the seat across from them. His fedora was tilted over his face, his hands laced together over a folded copy of the *Planet*. One leg extended out into the aisle, the toe of his shoe touching the back of the chair two rows in front of him. His suit hung loose over a bony frame, giving the appearance of a man stretched beyond normal dimensions.

"No, sweetheart," her husband said after some consideration. By his tone it was clear they had this sort of conversation often. "Foster Fade wouldn't be caught dead riding the train. Let alone second class. Probably has his own private airplane."

"Those exist?" the woman said in breathless shock, as if the Wright Brothers had just invented air travel that day.

"Oh, of course, dear," her husband said, suddenly eager to school his wife on the various mysteries of the world. "Folks like that have a private everything. Plane, boat, car, even a train, I'd imagine. But why ride the rails when you can soar through the sky?" He waved a hand in the air with flair. "I'd imagine Foster Fade even has a direct line to

Howard Hughes, comparing notes on all their gadgets."

The woman shook her head. "Such a strange man."

"Hughes?"

"No! Fade," she added under her breath. "Him and the Stevens woman… Have you read their articles? Going around, acting like some sort of… well, you know, one of *those*."

"Those what?"

"*Vigilantes*," she said with disgust. "It's all for show, I think. That whole Post Box Killer fiasco, how do we know any of that actually happened? For all we know the story was invented just to sell papers."

Her husband furrowed his brow; surprised his wife had a seemingly cognitive thought. "Well, I guess you have a point there."

"Oh, I don't need any help moving papers."

The husband and wife blanched as they turned to face to the redheaded man.

"Excuse me?" the husband asked, squaring his jaw.

The stranger tilted back his fedora with his thumb, a grin on his handsome face.

The woman's eyes fluttered and her pale face turned a few shades whiter. "You—You're…"

"Foster Fade? I should hope so; it's on all my stuff," Fade said pleasantly as he placed his newspaper and fedora on the seat next to him. He ran a hand through his lengthy hair and crossed his significant amount of legs. He looked younger than either of them expected, his eyes sparkling with a wicked genius. "But, we're moving away from the point. You handed me some pretty deep criticisms, which, if I were a sensitive individual, would have terribly wounded my pride, but I work in the news business and I'm made of sterner stuff. I'll just drink away my sorrows in a flood of tears over my typewriter. That is if I ever sat over a typewriter. I tried it once, but my fingers moved too fast and I broke the keys. I've never seen Din so mad…"

The woman opened and closed her mouth several times without producing a sound.

"Please don't take offense," Fade said holding up a conciliatory hand, eliciting a small metallic click from his wrist. "I love meeting my critics. Always makes for some stimulating conversation. Please, continue. You were in the middle of saying that the whole Post Box Killer affair was made up to sell newspapers. I'm *fascinated* to hear what evidence you have to support that theory, or a thesis, or whatever the right term is, I don't have a dictionary on me. Honestly, it's a miracle I can even speak English. So," he leaned on the seat in front of him, rested his cheeks on his hands and looked at them attentively, "enlighten me."

The woman pursed her lips, cleared her throat, and arched her back, her fur and feather coat bristling. It reminded Fade of a peacock, or a bull about to charge, or some strange chimera between the two.

"Kathleen," her husband said, suddenly panic stricken. He placed a hand on her knee. "Perhaps we should—"

"Mr. Fade," the wife said, undeterred. "I should have you know that I am the—"

"I don't care who you are, Kathleen. You could be the Queen of India for all I care. Though I'm sure you'd be a lot more fun if you were. They *really* know how to use their hips. Oh, don't be so prudish. Here, let me show you something." Fade opened his jacket revealing a complex patchwork of machinery wrapped around his chest like a robotic vest. He unhooked a palm-sized piece off and held it up, a thin wire strung to the device. "It's really quite impressive stuff, came up with it last week while I was… Well, let's just say I was neck deep in concrete at the time." His eyes focused on his memory. "Weird day…"

"It looks like a phone," Kathleen commented.

Fade smiled, brought back from his reverie. "Look at you! Not as thick as you look. It is a phone! It only calls one number and it weighs a ton, but it's completely portable. At least, with this vest. And there's a brace involved. And you need to switch out the battery every hour. But it's completely portable. It will revolutionize communication. If it works, that is. Spent the whole day testing the range. Went all the way up to Albany and now back. Mostly it's been… static. Lost my screwdriver up in Troy, which is an awful little town. Actually, and here's the funny thing, if you were to arrange the components incorrectly you'd get a pretty spectacular bomb, but don't worry, it's totally harmless like this. Just think of the possibilities! It's perfect for when you're traveling or in a spot of trouble and need help before you end up neck deep in… concrete, which, mind you, happens to me on the regular. And before you ask, no, I haven't thought up a name yet. I never think up names for these things. It would be like naming a child that was, you know, made of bibbly bits that winked and turned… Sorry, I'm getting away from myself. Din's the writer. I just talk."

Kathleen sniffed. "Clearly… Mr. Fade, I don't know who you

think—"

"Hey, I just paid you a compliment!" Fade said, clutching at his heart. "Besides, you haven't really answered my question, which I'll admit, is rather rude considering I'm going out of my way to show you all this exciting stuff! You don't have to get all prissy."

Kathleen slapped Fade across the face.

"Come on, George," she said sternly, grabbing her husband's hand and dragging him into the other car.

For his part her husband tipped his cap in apology. "Mr. Fade…" he said beneath audible levels.

"For the record private planes are really expensive!" Fade called after them. He hooked the handset back onto his belt and rubbed his cheek until the stinging went down. It always hurt more than he expected it to. He even felt a tear well up in his right eye. Why did that always happen? He had barely broken a sweat when he had been shot in the past, but a woman slapping him always made him tear up. He decided to blame physics.

There was a soft chuckle behind him.

He glanced to the bald man seated a few rows back. "I probably deserved that," he admitted with a shrug.

"I think you did, Mr. Fade," the bald man agreed with a pleasant smile. He looked nearly as tall as Fade, with a significantly more muscular frame. His head was a smooth as a cue ball, his face covered in the shadow at the back of the car.

"To be honest, I'm not even sure what I was trying to prove. Maybe I'm just feeling…" he trailed off, his eyes briefly losing focus. "Bitter."

"But it was an impressive show," the man offered.

"Always the entertainer," Fade said with a crooked grin. He fixed his fedora and tucked his long chestnut hair behind his ears. "I had originally planned on starting a vaudeville act, magic, gizmos, pratfalls and whatnot. Foster Fade, The Spectacularist. It would've looked great in lights. Then I went ahead and solved a crime—a murder if you were asking—and boom! The Crime Spectacularist was born. Don't tell anyone I told you that. It's all a lie. Or at least you can't prove otherwise."

"Not something you'd want in print?" the bald man asked conspiratorially.

"There are a lot of things I don't want in print. Hell, even the stuff I want in print gets me in trouble."

"I heard about that."

"Everyone's heard about that," Fade sighed, waving dismissively to the aether. "The *Sentinel*, the *Herald-Tribune*, hell, even the *Times* ate me alive. I couldn't even walk two steps without hearing my name on the radio. The studios want to make a picture about it. Not that I'll see a dime, mind you. They'll fictionalize it all, call it something ridiculous like 'Murder by Mail.' Which is not what happened by the way," he added with a wag of his finger. "It was lot more disturbing than that."

"No, I read the articles, Mr. Fade," the bald man said reassuringly. "I am a fan of yours."

Fade pinched his eyes shut. "Please don't say that. I have had enough of my fans already. I'd rather that Kathleen woman come back and slap me around a bit more than deal with any more of my fans."

"I'm sure she wouldn't mind either," the man said with a laugh.

"Well as long as everyone's happy."

The bald man leaned on the seat in front of him, his arms slung out, the silver and gold ring on his right middle finger glinting in the evening light. His face came into view. It was plain and unremarkable, unscarred and unblemished; brown eyebrows over empty brown eyes; a sloping nose, thin lips curled at the ends, high cheekbones and rounded chin. He looked young, perhaps no older than Fade; and save for the shaved pate and pale skin, there was nothing instantly identifiable about him. He could be just another face in the crowd, easily ignored and forgotten. "Can I ask you a question, Mr. Fade?"

"Only if it's 'a' question and not secretly 'several.' I'm hoping to get to the dining car before it closes so I can grab myself some ice and liquor. For my face and stomach, though I'm not sure which is which just yet."

"Why don't I join you then?" the man suggested, waving in the direction of the dining car.

Fade's eyes narrowed as he considered the offer. "Only if you agree to buy a round."

"It'll be the first."

Fade smiled, lightly patting the man on the back. "You are quickly becoming my best friend."

Chapter 2
CATCH AND RELEASE

FADE WATCHED THE liquor and ice swirl together in his glass. The drink was better than he expected, not that he ever had high standards for this sort of thing. Din obsessed about it, throwing away whole bottles of wine if the first sip didn't match her expectations. As long it got him toasty, Fade couldn't care less how it tasted.

He was seated diagonally, the tips of his shoes sitting in the aisle, which was probably a fire hazard he realized, but when was the last time there was a fire on a train? That sort of stuff stayed in the Old West, or at least in the films that purported to be about the Old West. He glanced out the window, watching as three small hills rattled by and felt suddenly nostalgic. "You know, I had a friend who grew up not too far from here," he said before he could stop himself.

The man smiled with genuine interest. "Is that so?"

"Yeah, little place called Black Rock," Fade said, sipping at his drink. He gestured at the small town flashing between the trees. "Not many people have heard of it. Doesn't even have a train station. Mostly just farms and a couple of municipal buildings so it can qualify as a 'town' and not a 'village.' I visited there a couple of times. It seemed nice."

"Grew up between the Three Hills, did he?" the man chuckled. He reached into his jacket pocket and pulled out a matchbook and a dented chrome cigarette case, the letter "X" engraved in the center.

"Right beneath Tinwood. Small little place, just him and his dad. You know, most people who get into my line of work, adventuring and detective-ing, I mean, they all have this weird childhood trauma. But, you know, I had it pretty good. But, my friend, from what he told me, he had it better than anyone." Fade shrugged. "Maybe I was even a little jealous of him. A happy childhood. Who wouldn't want that?"

"It's very rare," the man commented as he lit himself a cigarette and replaced his case. "I take it you're from there as well."

Fade frowned and waved his hand. "I'm from here and there. Never in one place long enough to call it home. There's a name for that. Or possibly a song, or both. Though I'm damn certain I've read a book about it once or twice."

"You probably have," the man said with a smile.

Fade took a thoughtful sip of his drink and realized they had shifted far from the matter at hand. "I don't think you asked me your question."

The man nodded. "I didn't."

"And here I am blabbing away, which, admittedly, is my wont. I usually tell people I love the sound of my voice and I'm afraid that is very much the case. Were I not in print I'd probably be telling my stories in the picture shows, which I'm sure one day will be in everyone's home sent wirelessly..." He absently patted at his jacket pockets. "Which I'm sure I have a schematic for on me somewhere..."

The bald man smiled. "There was an article I read a few months back, damned if I can remember the title. It was after, you know, that whole..." He twirled his hands.

Fade arched an exasperated eyebrow. "After the 'Murder By Mail,' you mean?"

The bald man took a quick swig of his drink and coughed. "After that. It was a bit different than your normal stuff, it was... Actually," he gestured out the window, "it was about Black Rock."

Fade hesitated only a moment before he snapped his fingers. "Ah, yeah. I remember that one. 'The Hollowed Out Mountain.' Right. Din and I wrote it... God, must have been a year before we printed it. Gubb held off on it saying it was 'too ridiculous' and 'didn't fit our standard.' Which, yes, is true, all of our articles are mysteries, crimes, murders and whatnot, but I insisted. There was a point to it, I told him. A method to my madness. Not that he listened, of course. Heck, even Din was skeptical, but I had her write it up anyway. So Gubb tucked it away, told me he'd save it for a 'rainy day,' as if Din and I would ever want for material. But, sure enough, the day came when we were one article short, and Din and I were... Actually, that was the day when we were kidnapped by the Lizard People... Actually, they weren't Lizards and they really weren't people... Good kissers, though. Now *that* was a really weird day. Anyways, Gubb had no choice but to drop it in or see his readership drop a couple of thousand."

"It was an interesting article."

A smile curled in the corner of Fade's mouth despite himself. "It was, wasn't it? If I remember it correctly, we talked about how the government was building a super-secret mystery lab beneath one of the hills surrounding the town. South Grand, I think." He took another swig of his drink, watching to see how the other man would react. "We only had a little bit of evidence, but my source was reliable enough for Gubb to let it through to print. I mean, a hollowed out mountain in Black Rock? I know my gadgets might seem like they're out of science fiction but... a hollowed out mountain? Come on. Even to me it sounds ridiculous. " The ice clinked against the glass as Fade sipped at his drink. "But, like I said, not really our normal stuff, but I had my reasons."

A cold smile formed on the man's face, his brown eyes empty. "How did you hear about it?"

"Ah, ah..." Fade wagged a reprimanding finger. "That's two questions."

"Only the first," the bald man corrected. "I never asked you anything. You just—"

"Talked. Yeah. I do that."

"So?"

"How did I hear about it?"

The bald man nodded.

"It's not that big of a mystery, really," he said eventually with a cryptic smile. "Loads of construction vehicles were flowing in and out of a town that, for the most part, hasn't been able to find its way out of the squatter camps. You'd think all those people itching to lift a shovel would've been hired on the spot, but nope, not a single local was hired. And when they were done nearly two years later there wasn't a single building built except for a small wooden cabin. Odd, don't you think? Plus, according to my source, who I trusted implicitly, they were shipping in these big ventilations systems, the sort they use in the Holland Tunnel and what use are those for a cabin in the hills?"

"And who was that? Your source, I mean."

Fade tapped the side of his nose. "A good reporter never reveals his sources. Doctor-patient, Lawyer-client privilege and such."

"Hm," the bald man sounded. "Are you sure you can't tell?" He asked, moving his hands off the table.

Fade leaned back in his chair and studied his companion for a moment while subtly tinkering with his right wrist. "Why do you want to know?"

The man shrugged. "Curiosity."

"You know what they say about that and the cat..."

"Mr. Fade," the other man said after several moments. "I sense you've become a little cold to me all of the sudden."

Fade stared at his drinking companion, his face like stone. "I never got your name."

"I didn't give it," the man replied with a smile, his eyes falling into shadow.

"And I take it you're not going to?"

A sharp metallic click sounded from beneath the table.

Fade's gaze instinctually dropped down. "Really?" he sighed.

"I'm afraid so," he replied, his voice hollow and his face hard.

"Well, this is an unpleasant turn of events," Fade commented, adjusting his tie. "And here I thought we were becoming friends."

"Who was your source at Black Rock?"

"You *actually* hollowed out South Grand?" Fade asked conspiratorially, but the man's expression was unreadable. Fade sighed, leaned back in his chair and laced his fingers together. "Well, look if you're going to kill me, which I assume is the logical end to this, could you at least tell me who you're working for or am I going to have to guess?"

The man stared at Fade for a moment. "Call it a collective of individuals who'd rather stay out of the papers."

Fade rolled his eyes. "I'm glad we're getting specific." He toasted and finished off the last of his whiskey with one quick swig. "Well, at least you bought me a drink."

The man nodded. "It was the polite thing to do. Now, if you would reciprocate."

"I'm afraid I'm going to have to be rude," he said evenly. "No offense, of course, you seem like a perfectly friendly assassin—probably the nicest I've ever met, and I've met a few."

"Must you make this difficult, Mr. Fade?"

"Of course." Fade nodded in assent. "You're not about to kill me right here, in front of all these people," he said, gesturing to the other passengers milling about the dining cart.

"Who says I won't just kill them as well?" the man replied with a dead voice.

Fade's eyes narrowed. "Well, then, you've just made this a lot easier." There was an audible click as Fade quickly flicked his wrist, ejecting a small pistol from the inside of his sleeve into his hand.

The man eyed Fade's pistol and smiled. "Hidden in your sleeve?"

"Designed it myself," Fade replied with a broad smile, sounding more thrilled with himself than was proper. "It only houses one shot, but at this range, it'll do the job. Honestly, I can't believe I'm getting a chance to use it again so soon."

"Hm. I should get one of those for myself."

"I'll take that as a compliment."

"You should."

"I guess this leaves us at an impasse."

The man arched a quizzical eyebrow. "Does it?"

"Well, not really," Fade said with bravado. "You see, I'm Foster Fade and I'm really quite famous. And not just poster-boy famous, though Lord knows I have the looks. I'm a hero, sometimes with a capital 'H.' The sort that weeds out villainy and all that ridiculousness. The Crime Spectacularist, they call me. I even have a billboard in Times Square. Hell, I could even have a fan club with one of those dumb secret decoder rings if I wanted."

"Which means…?"

"Which means, if people see me shoot someone, you can be sure they'll assume I'm in the right."

The man gave him a thin smile. "Is that so?"

Fade heard a soft pop from beneath the table and felt a sharp pain in his side. He glanced down at his stomach in shock.

"A silencer," the man commented off Fade's stunned expression. "That wasn't a kill shot, Mr. Fade, but I can promise you if you don't tell me what I need to know, the next one will be."

Fade didn't hesitate to fire.

THE HEAT RADIATED from Din's cigarette and filled her lungs, giving her a hint of relief. They kept it cold in the Arctic Lounge. They said it was better for the liquor and the aesthetic, but Din knew it was a holdover from Prohibition when the lounge was a speakeasy tucked inside a meat locker. Waiters snaked between the tables, serving trays filled with cocktails so complex they bordered on chemistry. It was still too early for dancers so the band played light, soft strings and horns, barely audible beneath the babble.

"You could at least look at me when I'm talking to you," Luke said, his brow furrowed to the point of being mountainous. He took a long drag of his cigarette, waiting to see if Din would respond.

Din tapped her cigarette into the ashtray, black, grey and red embers fluttering down like snow. She noticed the fingers on her left hand were tapping the air. She was writing again, just fifty keys short of a keyboard. "I'm sorry, were you talking?"

Luke let out a long sigh, cigarette smoke and frozen breath steaming. "I'm not even sure why I'm here."

"Because you choose to be." She took another drag and winced. She didn't mean to sound so cold. Luke had been courting Din off-and-on for the better part of a year. He was a crime reporter for the *Herald-Tribune*, though Luke sometimes moonlighted at the Amalgamated Press as a writer for the late-night news hour. Despite the round-the-clock lifestyle Luke was still fit and trim, and save for a thatch of grey on his right temple, looked no older than thirty. He had met Din some time after the firestorm that was the Post Box Killer and the two had gotten along well enough for Din to accept an invitation to dinner, out of curiosity if nothing else. She liked him usually, but the rest of the time her eyes and her mind seemed to wander, waiting for something to pop up around the corner; another murder, another crime, another *something*. "Sorry," she said sincerely, "that sounded more philosophical than I meant it to be."

Luke quietly tapped his cigarette into the ashtray. "Where are you right now?" he asked after a moment.

Upstate, Din didn't say. "Here. I'm here. I promise, I'm here."

Luke arched an eyebrow. "You promise?"

She smiled. "Promise."

"Then, can you tell me what this thing is?" He pointed to the large contraption piled in the center of the table. "Or are we just going to keep on ignoring it for the rest of the evening?"

Din scratched her temple. "It's Foster's… thing."

Luke nodded slowly. "Okay… And what does 'Foster's thing' do?"

Din arched an amused eyebrow. "Why are you asking?"

"Well, for one it's taking up most of the table, which will make dinner a lot more cumbersome."

"And two?"

"It's a giant pile of machinery never before seen this side of the sun! Also, I have nowhere to put my drink."

A waiter appeared, placing two drinks in between them. Din's was a cloudy brown, while Luke's was practically invisible. Din swallowed her drink and quickly puffed at her cigarette to block the aftertaste. "It's a phone," she said under her breath.

"That's a phone," Luke said, moving his finger closer to the mess of machinery as if it would make it more real. "It looks like a vest. From the future."

Din sighed; she couldn't believe she was saying this aloud. "It's a *portable* phone."

Luke pulled his hand away, and then pointed it forward again. "That's a phone? Seriously?"

"No, it's all one big ruse to bemuse and befuddle people," Din replied dryly. "I'm so happy it's working."

Luke opened and closed his mouth, trying to process the idea. "How is that a phone?" he eventually managed. "Doesn't it need wires and cables and um… other things?"

A low bell chimed from somewhere within the pile of machinery.

"Well, it rings," Din said pleasantly in response. "So that's half the battle."

Louis blinked slowly in befuddlement. "Aren't you going to answer it?"

Din smiled. "Unless you want to."

Luke reached for the small handset hooked to what looked like a belt before he stopped himself. "Who's on the other side?"

"Try and guess."

Luke withdrew his hand and returned to his drink, letting the phone ring. "He ever give you a night off?"

"I think a better question is, do I ever give myself the night off."

"You two act like a married couple," Luke said over his drink. "I often wonder if I should be jealous."

"It's not so complicated. He adventures, I write."

"But he gets the all the glory," he added pointedly.

"That's how ghostwriting works," she said. "All that matters is if my name is on the check. Dinamenta Stevens," she said, stabbing her cigarette into the air with each syllable. "And it's a very big check."

Luke chuckled. "Okay, now there I'm jealous. Maybe I should be a little more forward thinking and have you cover this one."

"Need a few more drinks in me before that can happen." She waved over the waiter.

"Anything else, Miss Stevens?" the waiter meekly asked.

"Nothing besides this," Din said, handing him her empty glass. "And twice as strong." She took a hard drag of her cigarette. "And for the fella here…"

Luke leaned back in his chair and took a patient drag off his cigarette.

"Why don't you surprise him?"

They let the phone between them continued to ring.

"Are you going to answer it?" Luke said with a nod.

Din smiled coyly. "Unless you want to."

FADE CLUTCHED HIS side, dark fluid leaking between his fingers, the phone's handset clutched between his head and shoulder as he kicked open the door to the next car. Behind him the rush of air and the sliding door cut out the screams of shocked patrons. "Din! Dammit, Din, pick up!" he shouted, the low warble ringing madly in his ear. Why on Earth had he thought this would be a good sound for phone calls? "Pick up the-phone!"

There was a pop and click of static and Fade felt a sudden tremor of panic just before he heard a voice crackle through.

"Hello?" the voice sounded distance, almost as if it was someone whispering from the bottom of a well. But impossibly, the phone worked.

"Din!" Fade nearly shouted with delight.

The male voice on the other end chuckled. "'Fraid not, Foster."

Fade stopped short and nearly fell over. "Who the hell is this?"

"Luke," the other man replied pleasantly. "Luke Jaconetti. We met a few months back during the—"

"Who?"

The other man cleared his throat. "Well, my pride's just been wounded a little. I think he wants to talk to—"

A brief rattle echoed through the line before Din's voice came on. "Hello, Fade."

"Din?"

Din let out a long electronic sigh. "Yes?"

"Din, it's me!"

"Who else would it be?"

"Who the hell is Luke Jaconetti?"

"Crime reporter for the—"

"It doesn't matter. Din, there's been a spot of trouble," he whispered as passengers watched him run by. He grabbed a large briefcase off the overhead rack, briefly stumbling from the weight. One man jumped up and cursed, fists clenched but Fade shoved him back into his seat.

"Am I supposed to be surprised?"

Fade struggled to unlock the door into the first class car, his hand slick. He rammed his elbow against the door handle to no avail. What he wouldn't give for his missing screwdriver. He moved to kick open the door when a bullet whizzed past his head, shattering the window. Fade spun away in time, covering his face with his arm. He glanced back and saw the assassin racing toward him, gun raised. "You know I could really not use the sarcasm right now!"

"And yet you called me."

Fade knocked away the remaining bits of glass in the window, reached through and unlocked the door. He felt another bullet zip past as he dove forward into the first class car. He landed hard on his back, briefly knocking the wind from his lungs.

There was something faint echoing beneath the static. Fade pulled the handset from his ear and eyed it suspiciously as he tried to identify the rhythmic tone that almost sounded like— "Is that music?"

It was several moments before Din replied. "Possibly."

"Where are you?"

"The Arctic Lounge."

"Are you—Are you on a date?"

Din hesitated. Din never hesitated. "No."

"Why would you be on a date when we're testing the… phone thing?"

"And look, it works!" she replied happily.

"Do you remember the Black Rock article?" he asked, ignoring her comment as he dropped to his knees, locked the door and propped the suitcase between the door and the wall.

"The what-what article?"

"Black. Rock. *Black Rock*," he barked in frustration as he crawled along the floor, testing the doors of each compartment and finding all of them locked. "Do you remember the article?"

"Wait… Wait… That was the one you had me write up because of— Wait. You mean the 'bait'?!"

"Yes!" Fade hissed.

"It worked!?" Din said excitedly, her voice ringing in Fade's ear. "You found him! You found the man who murdered—"

"Yes, and he shot me in the stomach!"

"How are you still alive?"

"The bullet ricocheted off the phone, busted the fluid reserve," Fade replied. He glanced down at the leaking canister on his side, thankful, not for the first time, he had designed the prototype as a vest and not a belt as he had originally planned. He wiped the oil off his fingers onto his pant legs.

"Why would a phone need a fluid reserve?"

"It's experimental," he said defensively.

"Then how are you talking to me?"

"Right now I'm willing to believe in magic."

"What about your friend?"

"I shot him."

"Is he still alive?"

Fade heard the cacophony of glass shatter and the smack of wood cracking as the assassin tried to force open the door. Fade risked a glance over his shoulder and quickly moved over to the next compartment. He had a minute, maybe seconds left before he broke through. "He was wearing a bullet-proof vest!" he hissed.

"That's why you always aim for the head."

"Oh, like you're such a good shot."

Fade worked open the compartment door and stumbled through to find it occupied by a couple in various states of undress. They quickly pulled on their clothes and voiced their panicked apologies before they realized it was Foster Fade standing before them.

"Ah, Mr. and Mrs. Kathleen. How are you?" he breathed as he locked the door behind him. "It seems you two are enjoying the ride."

"What are you doing in here, you monster?!" Kathleen gasped as she pulled her blouse over her chest. Her red lipstick was smeared across her pale face, like a shock of blood.

"I should ask you the same question, ma'am," Fade replied pleasantly, fixing his tie. "Don't you need a ticket for first class?"

"We're only one stop away!" Kathleen's husband stuttered.

Fade looked at him and frowned. "That's all the time you need? That's depressing."

Din's voiced crackled through the receiver. "Who are you talking to?"

"Some old friends. I'll call you back," he said before hooking the handset back on his vest.

"Get out of here!" Kathleen shrilled.

Fade clapped his hand over her mouth and held a finger over his. Her husband moved to protest but Fade clapped his other hand over his mouth as well.

"Mr. Kathleen," Fade whispered to the husband.

"George," he muffled a reply from beneath Fade's hand.

"Whatever. You look like a respectable man, a fan of the second amendment and all that ridiculousness. You wouldn't happen to have a firearm on you? Mine proved to be ineffective."

George puckered his brow. "Are you mad?" he breathed.

"Yeah, I thought it was a long shot. No pun intended. Okay, maybe a little."

"What are you doing here?" Kathleen moaned.

"Hiding," Fade whispered. "Did we not go over this? Sorry about that, I got caught up. Someone's trying to kill me, and believe me, I'm not doing this to sell papers. Suffice to say I'd very much like to play the quiet game right now. Winner gets a dollar."

Outside the compartment, Fade heard the last crash of wood as the assassin made his way into the car. Several seconds passed before Fade heard the slow, methodical creaking of footsteps walking up the corridor, briefly pausing at each compartment door. Spots began to form in front of his eyes and Fade discovered he was holding his breath.

There was another step, a creak of the floor, a knock on a door, and another step closer.

Fade felt his arms begin to quake, whether from exhaustion or fear didn't matter, he needed to remain stiff, a statue, silent and immobile. He pinched his eyes shut as his breath stuttered out his lungs. As a boy, Fade had read a lot of stories about heroes, men who would sacrifice themselves for the safety of others, who would face death with a smile or some other ridiculousness. Fade was not that sort of man. He very much enjoyed the daily discovery of being alive and would be remiss if his streak was suddenly cut short.

More footsteps, louder as they approached.

Fade glanced down at the light radiating from beneath the door and waited for the eclipse.

Just a matter of moments now…

Fade could guess the next set of actions. The shadows would pass, one foot at a time. The assassin would knock, two soft raps. Fade and his undressed companions would hold their breath and wait for him to walk past. But the assassin would come back, one compartment at a time and there would be a click of metal followed by the whisper of bullets. Fade was as sure as nitroglycerin made dynamite.

His eyebrows pricked up at the thought. He glanced over his shoulder at the window; the trees and hills had given way to metal and brick. No, he decided. The risks outweighed the benefits.

The shadows moved beneath the door, one at a time. They stood there for a breath, a heartbeat, before a soft knock came at the door.

"Mr. and Mrs. Kathleen," Fade murmured. "Now would be a good time to duck."

"What?" Kathleen breathed.

"Duck!" Fade shouted, shoving the couple to the ground.

There was no sound of gunfire, only the snap of wood followed by the clinking of raining glass as the window shattered. Fade covered his head, the tiny shards lancing at the back of his hands.

"Someone's shooting at us!" Kathleen shrieked.

"Your powers of observation never cease to amaze."

There were three more shots and Fade heard the familiar *click-click* of an empty cartridge. With moments to spare, Fade jumped up and knocked away the remaining bits of glass with his elbow. The assassin began slamming his body against the door. "Stay down!" Fade instructed as he threaded his leg through the window. "If he comes in tell him to meet me upstairs. Don't worry, he seems to be a nice assassin so he probably won't kill you."

"Upstairs? Upstairs where?!" George shouted.

"Where else?" Fade shouted back when he felt a gloved hand clamp down on his throat.

Chapter 3
TERMINAL

LUKE CHASED DIN toward the Lounge's exit. His gut and heart seemed to be at war with one another, twisting and thrashing with violent abandon. "Where are you going?"

"Where do you think?" Din replied without looking back over her shoulder. "To save Fade."

Luke opened and closed his mouth, unable to find a legitimate reason to protest but wanting desperately to find a way to convince Din to stay. He took a couple more steps toward the exit before he finally managed, "Din, I—"

Din turned around and shrugged. "Well, are you coming?"

Luke's mouth clamped shut. "Excuse me?"

Din gestured toward the door with the phone. "Are you coming? Lord knows what Fade's gotten himself into and I can't do this on my own."

It wasn't until Luke met Din's ice-blue gaze that he understood the offer, the equivalent of getting asked to join the Freemasons, Skull and Bones, and the Diogenes Club all at once.

Luke nodded brusquely. "Yes! Your car or mine?"

Din flashed a grin. "Mine, definitely."

"COME NOW, MR. FADE, you didn't think I would let you get away that easily?" the assassin growled as he pressed his gloved fingers down onto Fade's trachea while George and Kathleen cowered in the corner.

"I had hoped so, yes!" Fade choked as he struggled to free himself. Spots began to form in front of his eyes, little planets bursting into life. "That was a lie, actually," Fade admitted. "I was trying to lure you onto the roof of the train and give you some dramatic speech while I figured out a plan to defeat you."

"All I want is a name, a simple name," the assassin snarled, tightening his grip on Fade's windpipe.

Fade winced in pain. "I can't really answer... if you're... choking me."

The assassin whispered into Fade's ear, "Tell me and I will make this as quick as possible."

"Not quick enough!" Fade lifted his legs, kicked his feet against the compartment wall, and threw his body backward. Fade and the assassin tumbled through the door in tandem; wood, metal, and glass splintered into the air as Kathleen let out a warbling shriek. What little breath he still had left in his lungs shot out on impact, but the assassin's hold was broken. As the rainstorm of shards pounded down, Fade rolled away and stumbled to his feet.

"There's only one way you're getting off this train, Mr. Fade," the assassin said calmly as he stood, his sidearm already in hand.

"Come on, now!" Fade shouted. "If you were really going to kill me you already would have!"

"Mr. Fade, you're absolutely right," the assassin said with a smile, as he aimed the gun inside the compartment.

"THIS IS YOUR car?" Luke gasped.

"Yup," Din said nonchalantly as she tossed the phone on the back seat. The car was parked behind the Lounge, its smooth, streamlined ice-blue finish glinting in the twilight. The engine alone was the size of most sedans, the wheels—all six of them—capped with mirrored chrome, while twin metal piping ran off the engine beneath the driver and passenger doorways, leading into the swooping rear of the vehicle.

"It looks like an Auburn 8-100 Speedster, except with more..."

"Fade made the upgrades himself." She shrugged. "I think he was bored."

Luke pointed to the two cylinders placed above the back wheels. "Those are rockets."

Din nodded in assent. "Those *are* rockets."

"Those are rockets and they are on a car. Why are there rockets on a car?"

"To go faster," she replied as if she'd been asked whether two and two still made four. "Get in, I doubt we have much time."

"I wouldn't be surprised if you had a machine gun hidden in the engine," Luke said as he shut the passenger door behind him.

"Ha! Machine gun hidden in the engine. Don't be ridiculous…" She turned the key and the car roared to life. "It's in the glove compartment."

"What?!"

"Buckle up."

"NO!" FADE SHOUTED as he plowed into the assassin, knocking him down the narrow hall. "No one is dying today!"

Fade seized the assassin by the wrist and slammed his gun hand into the side of the car, once, twice, three times until the gun tumbled to the floor. The assassin grabbed Fade's phone vest and pulled him over. Without thinking, Fade unhooked the phone, slipped out onto the floor, snatched up the assassin's weapon and shot him the leg.

The assassin grunted in pain, spinning on his heel and limping away at a fast clip, Fade's phone still in hand. Fade watched as he threw open the car doors and climbed onto the roof.

"He stole my phone!" Fade said through gasping breaths. He wiped away the spit collecting at the corner of his mouth with his shirtsleeve.

"Mr. Fade…" Kathleen moaned behind him.

"Don't worry, I'll get him, Mrs. Kathleen… It'll just be—oh."

Kathleen lay on the floor, a deep wet spot of maroon on the side of her dress. Her husband cradled her head while pressing his hand against the bullet wound, blood leaking out between his fingers.

"I believe—I believe I was shot."

Fade kept his face calm. Please, not another death, not another death because of him… "You'll be all right, Mrs. Kathleen. Just fine, really. Looks like the bullet went through, which is always a good thing. Mr. Kathleen, could you put your other hand over… Yes, well, done, Mr. Kathleen!" Fade exclaimed, patting George on the shoulder. "Strapping man you are! Looks like we've got the right man for the job! Excellent. Kathleen, you're going to be okay." He said with a false smile. "Mr. Kathleen is going to hold down on the wound as hard as he can to stop the blood flow, and he's going to do it because he loves you. Isn't that right, Mr. Kathleen?"

"Yes. Yes, of course." George said, tears spilling down his cheeks.

"You two stay right here… I'm going to solve a five year old murder and make sure that man pays for this."

"Solve a murder?" Kathleen whispered. "How?"

"With wit and guile, Mrs. Kathleen!" Fade said with a thin smile. "Wit and guile."

DIN TORE THROUGH evening traffic toward Grand Central Terminal, running her car over sidewalks and through stoplights, ignoring the cries of pedestrians and whistles of police. It was just like Foster to get himself into trouble on a simple excursion. She couldn't even be afforded one night off with the man she was—Well, the man she was with. Luke wasn't wrong, not completely. Din's relationship with Foster was something close to marriage, deeper than friendship and spiced with near constant frustration. She liked him quite a bit, perhaps in some sense loved him in the way that life with him was almost, but not quite, as undesirable as life without him.

"Are you going to fill me in on whatever the heck is happening?" Luke shouted over the roar of the engine.

"I don't like to do exposition this late in the game," Din responded as she narrowly avoided an old nun. "Slows things down when there should only be action, action, action."

"Open up the machine gun so we can keep it interesting!"

Din snorted despite herself. "A few years ago a man very close to Fade died up in the small town of Black Rock. The death was ruled natural causes, but Fade was certain it was murder, so he planted a story that would draw the killer out of the woodwork."

"And I take it his plan worked."

"Oh, they always work… eventually, though sometimes I kind of wish they didn't."

There was a sudden flash of light followed by an audible bang that rattled the car.

"Holy hell!" Luke screamed, shielding his eyes. "What was that?!"

Din didn't bother to glance up at the fireball. "Take a guess!"

THE CITYSCAPE OF New York rushed by, the smoke filled air tossing Fade's long red hair over his face as Grand Central Terminal barreled into view. The assassin stood atop the train engine smiling, unaffected by the wind or swaying of the train, Fade's phone still in hand. Well, this was certainly making a mess of things. But at least it would make a fantastic story. Fade holstered the assassin's gun on his belt, adjusted his tie, and walked hopped on to the engine until he was only a few feet away from the assassin.

"For the record, coming up here was my idea first!" Fade said over the rush.

"All I wanted was a name, Mr. Fade. It would have been so much simpler if you had just given it," the assassin called back.

"Simpler?! Simpler how?!" Fade shouted back. "With an injection behind the ear? Make it look like I had a heart attack?"

The assassin tilted his head, but remained silent.

"You never needed to ask me his name! You already knew it!" Fade growled. "You knew it when you killed him five years ago. See, that's one thing you got wrong. You think you're hunting me? It's the other way round, buddy." Fade drew the gun from his belt. "I've been hunting you."

The assassin smiled. "Ah, so he did reach you did he?"

"Do you know who he was?! Do you know who he was to me?!" Fade screamed, pulling back the hammer. "He was the only family I had left!"

The assassin started to laugh. "Please, Mr. Fade. You won't kill me."

"I already shot you once."

"Ah, but you didn't aim at my head. A killer would have done that… I however…" He held up the vest and continued. "You thought I wasn't paying attention… You see, impressive as this is, I know it isn't *just* a phone. A little rewiring and it's also a bomb."

Fade's expression curdled. "You wouldn't."

"Wouldn't? I already did!"

Without a moment's hesitation, the assassin slid the vest across the roof just as the train barreled into Grand Central Station. Fade felt the heat before he heard the blast. The train car flew out from beneath him as metal twisted and glass exploded and the world turned into a subterfuge.

THE BLAST TORE the engine car in half, kicking the wheels off the rails. A tidal wave of panic ripped through the train as metal squealed and glass shattered, mixing with the passengers' screams. People and luggage were tossed around like glitter in a child's snow globe. In the cab, the driver was dead before he felt the flames. The train stormed toward Grand Central with an unmitigated fury. Several tons of brick erupted out as the train jumped off the rails at the end of its intended platform and plowed through the wall into the main concourse in a flurry of destruction. The train's wheels screamed against marble floors, echoing in the cavernous space, as the mechanized beast slid to a stop centimeters from the information desk.

Minutes passed. Inside the ruined platform powdered stone clouded the air, coating the space with unnatural silence.

Dizzy, Fade hung off the side of the train, his arm hooked in an open window. He dropped painfully to the ground, coughing up clouds of dust as he wobbled to his feet, eyeing the destruction around him with an overwhelming sense of what he would describe as proud embarrassment. A thin trail of blood ran down from his nostril. Fade absently wiped it away with his sleeve as he stumbled forward. He ran a hand through his hair and winced at the large welt at the back of his skull.

He walked over to a shattered compartment window and shouted. "Mr. and Mrs. Kathleen! How are you doing up there?"

An arm shot out from behind and clamped around Fade's throat. "In all my years, Mr. Fade, I've never dealt with someone as troublesome as you," the assassin hissed as he pulled Fade into the shadows. His face was singed a bright red, his once immaculate suit steaming from the heat.

"Thank you." Fade tried to worm his fingers between his throat and the assassin's arm, but the hold was too tight. Black and red splotches formed in front of his eyes, his lungs stinging. "Can't we just be really impressed you survived?" Fade grunted through choked breaths. "Because I sure am…"

The assassin tightened his grip. "If I can't get it from you, I'll just ask your pretty little ghostwriter—"

There was a sudden crack of gunfire, echoing in the dust. The assassin fell back and Fade collapsed to his knees, holding his throat.

"You stopped answering your phone," Din said as she appeared from the cloud, lowering her gun.

"He blew it up," Fade croaked in reply.

"Of course he did," Din sighed.

"You're late," Fade muttered as he dusted off his jacket.

"Glad to see you too," Din replied dryly as she placed her gun in her handbag. She nodded at the train wreckage. "Looks like you made a mess."

"You're surprised?"

"Wait, wait…" the man next to Din suddenly said, pinching the bridge of his nose. "I'm sorry, but I can only suspend my disbelief so far… How the heck did you survive?"

"Swung over the side just outside the blast radius. I'm a genius, remember? I know how big my explosions are going to be," he replied. He looked to Din and nodded to the man. "Who's this?"

"Luke," Din replied without expression.

Fade looked to Luke and furrowed his brow. "Who're you?"

Luke turned to Din. "Does he not know?"

The corners of Din's lips curled. "He knows."

Fade gave them a broad smile. "Oh, I know. Well, it's nice that she brought you along for moral support. Lord knows we need it… Now, to deal with our friendly assassin! Let's find out what's really going on in Black—" He spun around on his heel, stopping short when he found the space behind him void a body.

"Where did he go?" Luke asked.

Fade sighed. "Back under the mountain."

POLICE AND FIREMEN helped battered passengers climb out of the wreckage. Some were carried on stretchers, long florid wounds stretched across their faces, but the majority walked out on their own volition with little more than bruises to show for their trauma. Out in the main concourse dozens of pressmen and photographers shouted questions at the survivors and documented any information they could glean. Seated on a fallen stone, Fade watched the procession with mounting frustration.

"Gubb is going to kill us," he said for the tenth or eleventh time.

"Really?" Din retorted. "I could never imagine why."

"Is it always this exciting?" Luke asked deadpan.

Fade glanced over at him. "He's been hanging out with you too long, Din."

Someone, Fade wasn't sure who, kept insisting he wrap a blanket over his shoulders. It was only after the eighth attempt to remove it, that he gave up trying. He tugged the blanket closer over his body so he had something to do.

An hour passed—or at least it felt like it—by the time a familiar lieutenant approached. Fade recognized him from the Tipton Murders but still couldn't remember his name. "Mr. Fade, rumor has it you were involved with this ridiculousness," he said with a voice that reminded Fade of a pit-bull.

"Not by choice."

The lieutenant nodded. "Mm. I'll need you to chat with my boys in a few minutes, but I have a few questions I need to ask you."

"Make 'em quick, Lieutenant," he said sharply, finding himself suddenly missing Captain Stern's wine-stained mug. "Din's got to get back to the office so this story can make press. It's really important to her."

"Not my problem, Mr. Fade. And considering you gave me this one," he threw a thumb back toward the train wreck, "I'm going to keep you as long as I want."

Fade crossed his arms. "Ask away, lieutenant."

"Do you know anything about the couple in sleeping compartment?"

"Ah. Mr. and Mrs. Kathleen," Fade said brightly. "Nice folks. Apparently seem to really *enjoy* public spaces if you catch my—"

"Did you see who killed them?"

Fade's face steeled over. "Excuse me?"

"They were found in their compartment, both with a bullet wound to—"

"Show me."

The lieutenant brought Fade inside the tangled car, the walls and floor slanted and twisted like a funhouse. At the far end of the narrow pathway several police officers stood outside a compartment while a crime scene photographer set up his camera. The lieutenant had them all move aside so Fade could look inside. They were laid out together, side-by-side, the white sheets covering their heads as if they were sleeping. Fade could just see the collar of Kathleen's luxurious coat, the fur tramped down with a dark wet crimson.

"He came back and finished them off…" he said numbly.

"Who did?" the lieutenant asked.

Fade shook his head. "He didn't give his name."

"I could use a little more than that."

Fade turned to the lieutenant and began to tell his story.

"COME ON, WE have to get to the office and transcribe everything before I forget," Fade said with bravado as they left the station a few hours later. "We need to get this into the morning's paper. There's no way the Crime Spectacularist is going to be beaten by any of his illustrious competitors. Especially on his own story!"

"Foster," Din said softly behind him.

Fade stopped short, but didn't turn to face her. "You two look good together," he said after a moment.

Din's powder white cheeks turned an uncharacteristic ruddy. "You know that's not what I was going to ask."

"Let's pretend it was," he said quietly.

Din nodded in understanding.

"Who was he? The man who died up in Black Rock? Who was he to you?" Luke asked.

Din looked to Fade, who smiled distantly. "His name was Michael. He was a childhood friend. The closest thing I had to a brother. He was 'good to be good,' the sort of man… Well, the sort of man I try to be."

"And how do you think that's been going for you?" Din asked.

"Lieutenant! Lieutenant!" a sweating, rotund officer shouted as he plowed into the station. "There's been a gangland shooting at the navy yard! Five dead! And the eyewitnesses! You won't believe who's there!"

Fade looked back over his shoulder at Din and gave her a distant smile. "Let's find out."

THE END

FOSTER FADE'S BULLPEN

ABOUT THE AUTHORS

ADAM LANCE GARCIA was one of the youngest New Pulp writers when he exploded onto the scene in 2009 with his first novella Green Lama: Horror in Clay. Written as a gift for his father, Horror in Clay was nominated for Best Short Story in the 2009 Pulp Factory Awards. Adam's follow up novel, Green Lama: Unbound, took away two 2010 Pulp Factory Awards: Best Novel of the Year and Best Interior Art (thanks to the artwork of his frequent collaborator, Mike Fyles).

Hailing from Brooklyn, New York, Adam was raised on a high quantity of golden age comic books, movie serials, and Star Wars. Adam credits this atypical upbringing to his passion for writing.

He is currently writing several licensed properties at a number of publishers, including Moonstone Books, Pro Se Productions, and Airship 27 Productions as well as working on his original graphic novel Sons of Fire with artist Heidi Black.

DERRICK FERGUSON is from Brooklyn, New York. Married for 28 years to the wonderful Patricia Cabbagestalk-Ferguson who lets him get away with far more than is good for him.

His interests include but are not limited to: radio/audio drama, Classic Pulp from the 30's/40's/50's and New Pulp being written today, Marvel/DC fan fiction, Star Trek in particular and all Science Fiction in general, animation, television, movies, cooking, loooooong road trips and casual gaming on the Xbox 360.

Running a close second with writing as an obsession is his love of movies. He's currently the co-host of the Better In The Dark podcast where he and his partner Thomas Deja rant, rave and review movies on a bi-weekly basis.

Derrick Ferguson is best known for his Dillon series of adventures; Dillon and The Voice of Odin, Dillon and The Legend of The Golden Bell, Four Bullets For Dillon and Dillon and The Pirates of Xonira. For Pro Se Press he's written The Adventures of Fortune McCall. He has stories in various Airship 27 anthologies such as Mystery Men (& Women) Vol. II & III, Dan Fowler, G-Man Vol. II and Sinbad-The New Voyages.

AUBREY STEPHENS is a retired teacher from Mississippi. He has degrees in both theater and history, with certification in English, science, and special education. He is also a marine veteran and former military officer. The rumor that he has attempted to blow up the earth is just that, though he was on combat missile crew alert when the NORAD radar had a 65 cent computer chip fail and report that there were Soviet inbound missiles headed for the U.S. He is a trained martial artist with a second degree black belt in karate, brown belt in judo, and brown belt in Kendo. He also studied and taught European fencing for over 45 years. His hobbies include recreating the Middle Ages and the American Civil War. He is squired to one of the S.C.A.'s most well known knights and at this time holds the rank of Regimental Sgt.Maj. In the 3rd Tn. Cavalry Reg. He has acted, written, directed, or done set design and construction for over 200 theatrical shows. He has written several articles on the history of the War Between the States for regional magazines. Since his retirement from teaching he has edited for Pro Se Productions and will be a published writer with Pro Se soon as a part of their PULP OBSCURA imprint. He is in the process of writing a novelization of a golden age comic hero for Pro Se as well as working on an alternate history novel that stems from a slight change during 15 seconds in 1968. He enjoys swapping stories of the many sci-fi/fantasy conventions where he has worked, attended or been a guest. Stop and visit with him.

H. DAVID BLALOCK has been writing speculative fiction for nearly 40 years. His work has appeared in novels, novellas, stories, articles, reviews, and commentary both in print and online. Since 1996, his fiction has appeared in over two dozen magazines including Pro Se Presents, Aphelion Webzine, Quantum Muse, Shelter of Daylight Magazine, The Harrow, The Three-Lobed Burning Eye, The Martian Wave and many more. His current novel series is the three book Angelkiller Triad from Seventh Star Press. He served as editor for parABnormal Digest from its inception until the end of 2012. For more information visit his website at www.thrankeep.com.

DAVE WHITE lives in Lemont, Il, is married to his lovely wife Karen, and has two kids named Brandon and Allison, and a dog named Snickers. He dabbled with writing in his twenties when he was into Stephen King, but never pursued it. He discovered Pulp about six years ago, and with it a renewed passion for writing. He finally had his first story published in 2012 from Pro Se, and this year added an Avenger tale from Moonstone. He hopes to add many notches to his belt in the future.

Made in the USA
Lexington, KY
02 June 2016